A Long Ride

Razor

Book 2: A Long Ride

Henry Roi

I couldn't come up with a response before she deafened me with the 429's Flowmaster bellow. I put my helmet on and turned the choke off, tapped my machine in gear, foot stiff, calf still healing. Idled out onto the avenue and braked, facing Highway 90. Blondie backed out, turned and lined up next to me and rolled down the passenger window. The Ford's fresh coat of deep purple had been wet sanded and buffed to a mirror finish, reflecting the Hayabusa, the rider in black. She grinned at me, then held her hands up in front of a dash vent and sighed theatrically. Rolled up the window.

We were still in the process of breaking in our neighbors. You know, marking our territory. Our morning tradition was my favorite part of the day. We revved our combined 800 hp, then, like one mind we engaged our clutches and gunned the throttles. The earth quaking roar and smoldering black marks we left behind were sooo let-me-hit-it-doggy exhilarating.

Highway 49 was only a short jaunt up the beach. We hung a right there and weaved through ridiculous traffic, spotted the gym and turned into the drive. Shocker's El Camino and Ace's Scion blinged cleanly in the parking slots out front, among about fifteen other vehicles. We parked and went inside.

My hands and face began to defrost as I soaked up the exercise-heated air. I rubbed my fingers, turned baleful eyes on Blondie. She bobbed her head to the music pervading the wide room of exercise machines. *Too Close* by Alex Clare provided motivation for the early morning gym rats. Weight machines and barbells tinked and clanked. Treadmills hummed, footsteps thumping conveyor belts. Men and women grunted and breathed heavily. It felt like home.

Blondie took my hand and led me through the maze of equipment. She said hello to the muscle head that stood behind a tall counter sipping a protein shake while talking on the phone. Doug was immense, with a shaved head and too much spray tan. He looked at me and didn't blink, continued talking as if I didn't exist. His eyes moved to the blonde goddess in tights and his mouth snapped shut, teeth clicking, eyebrows racing to his hairline. He straightened to make sure she noticed his size, grinning, waved his shake. His eyes followed her ass as we walked past him into the back room.

"Come on! Move your butts!" Shocker yelled from the corner of the boxing ring. She saw us, glared *Hello*, and looked at the stopwatch in her hand. "Time!" she told the guys in the ring, two black teenagers that were soaked and gasping for air, barely able to stand after the pace the girl-beast had set for them. "To your corners, guys. You have one more round," she growled, reminiscent of our old coach.

They nodded to her, walked to their corners, sucking in deep breaths as if they were about to die. Stools had been placed in their corners by fellow boxers, a Mexican and white dude waiting their turn to spar. The exhausted fighters sat and peered out of their headgear to see who was watching their performance. About a dozen people were in the room. Mostly guys. Three girls, including Shocker and Blondie. Jump ropes whirled like whips and heavy bags boomed like bass tubes. Several people seemed more focused on Shocker than on their own workouts. She had the coaching thing down pat, which was uncommon; talented boxers usually don't make good coaches. This girl's confidence and *look* radiated Alpha Bitch in an intense way. And she pulled it off while looking great.

The fighters in the ring saw Blondie at the same time. She was facing away from them, stretching while talking to Bobby and Ace, her statuesque bod riveting their attention-and one by one the attention of all the men. Those not paying attention to Shocker's commanding presence had taken acute interest in my girl's twisting, bending form.

Shocker glared at her trainees, turned to see what had captivated them. She looked to see how I was taking it. I shrugged, *Comes with the territory*, and we laughed together.

She yelled to my girl, "Hey Blondie! You look like a naked black girl in those tights. How about standing ringside so my guys will double their effort?"

Blondie turned and waved at Shocker, still pointing her ass at the men. "Nah, there's enough testosterone in this joint already. Let's not stir up any more. We may have to hurt these guys."

The third girl, an early twenties brunette with a coltish build, flexed her arms and mugged *Bring 'em on!* while everyone in the room laughed. Some of the men held their hands up in surrender.

Shocker called time and coached her boys' final round. I grabbed Blondie's gym bag and went into the men's room to change. Shorts and tank top, both gray. Some old Grant boxing boots that came up mid-shin. White with red soles and laces. Put the bag in a locker with my clothes and went to take care of business.

Bobby was working with Ace in front of a wall of mirrors. They both wore black warm up pants and blue camouflage tees, matching Shocker's outfit. *What's up with the exercise uniform?* Bobby stood behind the geek and coached him on proper form with dumbbells. Ace banged out some lateral raises, teeth gnashed, shoulders burning, Big Swoll spotting his last three reps. Ace gasped in relief, dropping the weights on the rubber mat. "Fried circuits!" he cursed, grabbing his shoulders.

Blondie was shadowboxing a few feet away, watching herself in the mirrors, aware of all the eyes in the background and loving the attention. I stepped beside her and launched into a series of jabs to stretch my arms and torso, then proceeded to beat the crap out of my reflection.

I didn't particularly care for shadowboxing; it was sort of boring. But it was an essential exercise for all fighters. You had to do it if you wanted to maintain fundamental skills and rhythm. Eddy was a stickler for it. He used to tell his boxers, "If you don't do anything else, run and shadowbox." He preferred for us to shadowbox before and after a grueling workout, whether we were training for a fight or not. The discipline sticks to you after so many years. Every morning, six days a week, I run and box my shadow. Usually as a warm up, though sometimes it's all I do.

My reflection was fast. I stepped up the pace and matched him blow for blow, stepping with every punch, weight in the center, then over my front foot as I shifted out to jab and hook. I mixed up the angles, pivoting left and jabbing, dipping down, double uppercutting the body.

Pivoted right, throwing quick straight-rights and overhands. When I backed away from my reflection my hands were high, slapping down phantom punches, head weaving, slipping. I feinted jabs, throwing hard, fast straight-rights behind them. Then ripped combos to the head and body, over/under patterns that constantly changed so my opponent wouldn't know what to expect. Two to the head, one to the body. Three upstairs, two to the gut. Blazing jab to the face, powerful right to the belly, shoulders twisting explosively, legs thrusting me forward a split second before I tightened my fist against my shadow's form.

After about ten minutes I was breathing hard, sweat running down my sides, sufficiently warmed up. I stopped and bounced on my toes, conscious of the uncomfortable burn and *tug* in my left calf, which wasn't anywhere near 100% yet. I think some nerves had been damaged. Injuries like this take a very long time to heal, if they ever do. The neural connections have to find new pathways between brain and muscle. *Good thing it's not my right calf,* I thought. I fight off my back foot. A weak back foot is devastating to a boxer.

Blondie grunted out one last quick combo, stopped and grabbed a jump rope. Without break she began hopping foot to foot, spinning the plastic beads impressively, blue and white blur whistling over her head and under her toes with perfect timing and expert eye-hand-feet coordination. The mirrors showed her long ponytail flopping behind a determined face, breath rhythmic, boobies bouncing deliciously. She stepped around quickly, lithely, showing off moves she learned at dance clubs. Her effortless grace combined with her curvaceous form was intoxicating.

"Keep staring like that and Bobby might have to catch you again," the Shocker said, suddenly at my side. I looked at her. She punched me in the shoulder. "Come on, stud. You said you were working today."

"I am," I said, reluctantly dragging my gaze away from the sweaty goddess. "Working" meant sparring in boxing-ese. We walked toward the ring, passing Big Swoll and Ace. They were still slinging the dumbbells. One-arm rows. Great mass builders. Bobby's freakish forearms bulged, his left noticeably smaller, a result of the fractured radius he got catching my unconscious body.

I couldn't believe I passed out while repelling down the garage. I fell like twenty feet. For once I'm glad Blondie didn't listen to me and waited instead of leading everyone to our emergency rendezvous. They saw me fall. Big Swoll was close enough and strong enough to catch me. Likely saved my life. For sure he saved me from future wheelchair races.

I felt uncomfortable around him now. Not just because I felt indebted for my spine, but because he had to pull out of the bodybuilding contest he trained so hard for. And look at his arm. It was just now able to hold weight again. The old me wouldn't have given it any thought. *Keep thinking like a lame and the girl-beast is going to tie you into a gay bow...*

"Let's work," I said to the boxing legend. I began visualizing us already fighting, prepping my cortex, taking slow deep breaths to influx my muscles with oxygen. The drug came on hard, sharpening my senses to a laser fine precision. I ducked under the ropes, stepped into the battle zone.

"Biatch!" she taunted, throwing her signature blurring combo. Her hands had tracers as she gave me an exaggerated angry face. She nodded, *That's what's up*, and climbed up the steps, ducked under the ropes behind me.

Blondie and Ace took a break to attend to our gear. The red Ringside Products hand wraps went on quickly, Blondie's experienced fingers deftly winding the bone supporting material around my knuckles, through my fingers, compiling the last of it around my wrists. Ace was apparently a veteran of wrapping his wife's fists; he finished before Blondie.

Dude probably has a calculus formula for it, my subconscious chuckled.

Shocker and I stepped into jock pads that fitted thick foam over our clothes, the bands securing around our waists and legs, making my junk claustrophobic.

This shit again? My Johnson shifted in complaint.

Shocker's apprentices emerged from a gear room holding two sets of 10 oz. Ringside gloves, blue with Velcro wrist straps. They tossed them to Blondie and Ace. Our significant others put them on our hands, pulled the straps tight. I loved the feel of my bound, hard fists inside the light gloves.

Tools… I love my tools.

Next came the headgear, also blue, thick foam that encased our entire heads in protective cushion. The padding was low on the forehead and high on the cheeks, which limited peripheral vision but prevented cuts. I couldn't stand headgear, and normally wouldn't wear it. But sparring with a master like Shocker made me swallow my pride and allow Blondie to stuff my arrogant head into its protection.

Blondie gave me a good luck pinch on the nose. It hurt badly – my eyes watered. She put my mouth guard in. Stepped out of the ring in "my" corner. I looked across the twenty foot square circle and saw Ace put his girl's guard in. He ducked under the ropes, stood behind the corner post and held up his stopwatch, fiddling with the buttons. The girl-beast bounced on her toes, shaking her arms out. I did the same, taking deep breaths to quell the jitters in my stomach. Why am I so nervous?

Because this girl could very well hand you your ass, some prick's voice said.

Shocker glanced at her trainees. They watched her with pure adoration. They would absolutely shit their shorts if they knew who she really was. She pumped a glove at them, *Watch and see how it's done, boys,* then yelled at me, "Hundred and ten percent, Mister President! We have to set the bar for these guys."

"Ten percent body, one-hundred percent brain," I replied.

She looked at the four young men standing ringside. "Remember what I told you about boxing being more mental than physical?" They acknowledged. "What you'll witness here is that I won't be able to out punch this guy." She leaned over the top rope toward them and winked conspiratorially. "I'll have to out *think* him."

Bobby's booming chuckle overrode the younger men's.

Uh-oh. She seemed mighty confident. This chick had years of experience fighting in the pros, on a world-class level. Her credentials were intimidating. Our previous match was a real fight, and it could be argued that she won. I'm five inches and forty pounds bigger than her. But she isn't human. I've lost fights before, and I'm not scared of her, exactly. I was only worried about the embarrassment of losing to... *What? What is she to me?* Hopefully I won't get slapped around too much before I can adjust to her game.

Ace looked at me. "You ready?" he said with an excited smile. I nodded. Shocker turned and blew him a kiss. He thumbed the watch. "Time!"

"Let's go Baby!" Blondie encouraged. "Work behind that jab! Keep her on the end!"

The part of my brain that maintained a constant sense for music alerted me to the commercial break ending on the radio. I brightened for a second, anticipating the motivational drive a good rock song usually evokes. But someone had changed the station. The elation came crashing down as Alicia Keys started her build up to *This Girl Is On Fire.*

As you know, I believe everything is better with a song that fits the setting. I like this song. But it fits *her* setting.

"Bitch," I breathed, cursing the Odds.

As I feared, Shocker took heart from the jam, and with her gain came my loss-of testicles. They put on drag slicks and nitrogen raced into my stomach somewhere. I realized I was supposed to be watching her gloves and head, her "box," focusing on her hands to react defensively, eyeing her head for offensive strategy. Her compression sleeve held my attention, however. It seemed to glow like iridescent scales in response to her energy. Exo-skin. The Shocker stepped in a circle ripping off jabs that looked like a blur of reptilian strikes. "I love this song," she mumbled around her mouth guard, a pink horseshoe of rubber with tiny white lightning bolts for teeth.

She came out of nowhere. *Pap-pap-pap-pap!* Her speed was such that the combination resounded like a single blow. I snapped a right-hand, blinking as it sailed by her weaving head, eyes shutting tightly as she looped an uppercut under my arm, into my chin. "*Mmm!*" That was sneaky.

I pushed away so I could use my reach, attempt to keep the speed demon on the end of my punches, prevent her from darting to the inside. I feigned some jabs to see which way her head would jump, getting a sense of timing. Then faked again, throwing a hook where I thought her head would be. *Bip!* The fast light blow touched her headgear. The feeling of achievement was short-lived. She fired right back, popping me in the nose with an overhand counter. As I lifted my arms to push her away she was already under them, ripping loose a three piece to my stomach and ribs.

"Oof! Arrrmmm!" I said to her, spittle ejecting.

"Practicing your Vietnamese?" she queried breathlessly, banging her gloved fists off my arms, shoulders, not really trying to find an opening, just keeping something on me. "That was pretty good. It means 'Ow,' right?" She shoved away to recover.

I followed, smiling at her trash-talk. *She earned the right,* I conceded. Can't deny her that. I said, "Behind this frustrated, no-way-a-girl-is-getting-out-on-me face, I'm actually very impressed. I haven't seen combinations like yours in years."

"What can I say?" She pivoted and faced Ace, put a glove on her hip. "I give good combo."

He exhibited a lame blush. Bobby and Blondie voiced their pleasure, though the teenaged men reacted with stares and unintelligible mutters, infatuation locked into a higher gear. Shocker was putting on a show, and I felt cool for being a part of it.

Gay bow, my subconscious chuckled. *Gay. Bow.*

"This girl is on FIIIRRRE!" Alicia screamed beautifully, foreshadowing my opponent's next moves. I stretched my jab out in rapid succession, chasing her, seeking a range for my right-hand. She ducked, slipped, slapped down my gloves, having to really get busy under my assault. Exclamations from bystanders overwhelmed Blondie's and Ace's fostering from the corners.

Suddenly, she weaved and was under my arms, at my side, exploding off her back foot and banging a looping-right into my padded ear. She pulled the punch at the last instant, taking her time, letting me know she could have hurt me if she wanted to. She was toying with me, trying to get me irritated and out of rhythm. *It's working*, I thought, then complained, *How can a girl move that fast???* It wasn't natural.

"Time!" Ace shouted, putting a stool down for his girl. She sat. He wiped her face with a towel and gave her some water while she pumped a glove at the applauding crowd.

"You have to change your style," Blondie told me as I sat. She took out my mouth guard. Bottle fed me water loaded with epinephrine. "Don't go offensive like you usually do. Lay off the seek and destroy. Let her come to you and counter."

"But that's her style," I said.

She wiped my face with a thick beach towel. "It won't be if you do it too. Trust me." I looked at the words on her shirt. She grinned. "If you wait, she'll go offensive. Hook her."

She told me this with the conviction of feminine instinct, serious business. It sounded better than the confused no-plan that I had. "Bitch," I agreed. I touched my gloves to her boobies, bumped them up, down, in the center. She swatted my head, climbed out of the ring with the stool and water.

We stood. Ace yelled time. We shuffled to the center of the blue mat and touched gloves. Round Two. We circled, sweat beading on our arms, faces. It sucked to be bested by a chick. It was a blow to my ego in the worst way. But being schooled by the Shocker wasn't completely unpleasant. It was actually fun, I realized. What I imagine being outwitted by a sister feels like. A charge of euphoric amphetamine power blasted through me, lifting my gloves.

Armed with Blondie's intuitive advice, I circled and feinted instead of launching at her with a mad dash of jabs. Patient chess player rather than *blitzkrieg* hothead.

Shocker looked from my gloves to my eyes, suspicion glaring. *You can't fool me*, her piercing gaze said. She stopped moving, then crouched with her gloves high, stepped toward me slowly. Stalking. Liquid ripples of muscle. A big cat getting closer to her prey before pouncing. Her explosive one-two started at her back foot, crouched legs springing like a catapult throwing its shot of fists right at me.

I had been waiting on her move, but was nearly too baffled by it to execute my own. I countered as soon as she lunged, shifting to my left, her gloves grazing my right cheek, throwing a left-hook that tagged her in the forehead pad. It was a game of Beat Her To The Punch.

Speed! *Go! Go! Go!*

I pivoted left, already throwing an uppercut. It brushed her nose, her uppercut brushing mine. I pivoted back right, feigned a right-hand, then pivoted slightly to the left while throwing a hook. It compressed into her cheek pad with a satisfying squish of air.

We backed off, recovering.

It was so focused on the girl-beast that I was late sensing the crowd around the ring. It was larger. News of our match had traveled into the other room. Seven or eight more people, including the spray tanned hulk Doug, were grouped together outside the ropes, opposite the trainees. They smiled broadly, some cheering the Shocker, whom they knew as Anastasia. Only Blondie cheered for me. A few watched in quiet amazement, having never witnessed human beings move as we did.

Shocker gave me a gloved salute, acknowledging me as the winner of that exchange, then shook the same glove with a different glint in her eyes. *You got that one, but you won't get another.*

We'll see about that, I mugged back.

Controlled ferocity. I lunged at her with hands blazing, throwing combinations at five punches per second. "Shoe shining," as the old coaches call it. My light shots *popped* off her gloves, arms, slipping through her defense only once in twenty punches. She looked like a mongoose weaving away from a cobra, biding her time for the death blow. *Damn she's slick...*

I paused, guard up, sensing her imminent attack, poising for a counter. In the split second before she lunged I relaxed the tension in my shoulders and blanked my mind, trusting my much faster sub-conscious to sense her moves and respond. A blue tracer pumped at my head in a double jab. I moved quickly, though perceived it at a slower rate. I flowed backwards, skipping both feet at the same time, left glove slapping down her straight-right, arms and legs relaxed, eyes stretched wide to see everything at once. An ecstatic, rushing energy continued to flare through my stomach and limbs. I was in the zone. Ready to snuff her fire.

Her slow mo' punches drifted toward my face, ribs, easily blocked or slipped. She feinted a jab, and I intuitively knew she would throw a right-cross behind it. It propelled toward me with frustrated heat, and I briefly exulted in my ability to fluster the legend. *Uh-huh, got her out of rhythm, motherfucker!* As her punch reached the end of its range, an inch from my nose, I fired a right hand, following her retracting arm, glove thumping her forehead pad.

"Err-*uh!*" she snarled.

I didn't stop to pose. She was on me like a pimp beating a hooker. I ducked and caught her shots on my shoulders, arms, her onslaught so dynamic and surgical that I was forced to resort to desperate, un-orthodox tactics to break her focus. "I'm sorry baby!" I screeched in a ghetto accent, a terrible imitation of a battered prostitute. "I won't do it again. I'll bring yo' ya money!"

She backed off, dropped her guard, threw her head back, gasping laughter. I turned and strutted along the ropes like I had on heels and a skirt, walking on tiptoes while pulling my shorts tight around my ass. I glanced fearfully over my shoulder at the wrathful pimp. She found her breath and joined the crowd's loud laughter.

"Time!" Ace giggled.

Shocker walked to her corner. Sat and gave a good humored glare. "You're an ass!" she shouted.

"Thanks for noticing." I rubbed my glutes. Turned and showed her. "I do squats." She threw her water bottle across the ring. I ducked right before it hit me in the face. The Evian beverage rebounded off the middle rope, water gushing everywhere.

Blondie wiped drops of water from her face. "Told you," she said as I sat down.

"Yeah. It worked. Good coaching, Lean Meats." I drank greedily from the bottle she put to my lips. "I'll have to start calling *you* Strategos." She put my mouth guard in, and I lifted my gloves to touch her boobies. She knocked them down and hooked my headgear in one motion.

We bounced to the center, tapped gloves. It dawned on me we were going three minute rounds. Most females box two minute rounds, which is Blondie's preference. I recall several magazine articles that made the Shocker out to be a crusader, a pioneer for equal rights in the sport. Her efforts helped get women's boxing into the Olympics, and, if I remember correctly, she was one of the first women to have three minute rounds in a title fight.

Ask her later, my subconscious chimed in. *You know, after you've bested her and got our mojo back.*

If score cards were being kept, we'd be tied, each winning a round. I didn't plan on sparring all day. I was uncomfortably aware of her conditioning being superior to mine. She still trained like a pro athlete. If I challenged her to even a six rounder she'd wear me out down the stretch and show off. *We'll make this the tie breaker,* I decided judiciously.

"Last round?" I said.

"Sure. But if you make me look like an angry pimp again, I swear I'll tell everyone you whimpered like a sissy when Perry stitched your leg."

"No I didn't!"

"Yes you did."

"You just told everyone!"

"No I didn't."

"Yes you did!"

Ace yelled time but we were laughing so much we could hardly get in motion. The crowd was certainly enjoying the show. Just when I was shaking off the humor and reapplying my game face, the tug in my calf morphed into a searing, tearing *rip*. I fell on my butt, leg in the air, whimpering like a sissy. "O wow ow!"

The girls were at my side instantly. Blondie looked at the scars on my leg acutely, rubbing around them with tenderness. It burned badly, inflammation beginning to show under her long slim fingers. Shocker looked me in the eyes, shaking her head with sympathy. She said, "The ligament wasn't ready for so much excitement yet. Too bad." She leaned over and thumped a glove on my unprotected stomach.

"Armm-*grrrr!*" I sputtered, glaring.

Amused by my discomfort, she continued. "I would have dusted your squat-enhanced ass, you know that, right?" She stood and danced around in a circle, gloves above her head, a champion crowned. She threw a blazing combination. "This girl is on FIIRRRE!" she sang surprisingly well, gloves punching an azure blur.

"Wouldn't not," I wheezed.

"Would have to ooo," was her melodious response.

"Boss, you want me to carry him?" Amped from his workout, Bobby's voice rumbled louder than usual.

"Yes," the girls said together, not trying to hide their eagerness to see me carried like a bitch. Blondie took my headgear off.

"No. What?! No. NO." I shook her hands off. Grabbed a rope and pulled myself to my feet. Used my teeth to unstrap my gloves, mumbling, "My leg is fine. Just didn't warm it up enough."

The girls just looked at me. *Uh-huh*, their lifted brows and twisted lips implied.

Son of a biker whore. I knew what the burning in my leg meant: I had torn something I really need, a tendon or ligament that had been holding on by a thread. I had a feeling I needed surgery, and cursed myself for stressing my calf. I knew better, but just couldn't show weakness in front of my crew. I looked down. "You sorry bitch," I accused the injury. Then shrugged and forced the grimace off my face, let the pain become part of the high.

Blondie strained to pull the tight compression sleeve back over my lower leg, stood and patted my arm. Handed me the water bottle.

Shocker strutted across the ring and gave her man a sweaty kiss, both of them sporting huge smiles. Ace climbed through the ropes, kissed her again, and walked over to me. Pointed at my leg. "I can make you a better sleeve for that."

I looked at him hard. "No shit? EAP's like on her arm?" I glanced at shocker's arm sleeve.

He nodded. "I have a prototype ready to go, actually. My first leg piece." He put a hand to his chin. "We'll have to fit it and run the Intuitive program, but that won't take long."

He was being modest about it, though I knew it was a big deal. This tech won't be on the market for another decade. "So, what, I just walk around with it on?"

"Exactly. It will remember how you walk, run, jump - minutely - and will contract to assist those movements. It's controlled by a tiny processor with very sophisticated software."

"You have an extra Power Felt top?"

He shook his head. "A top wouldn't be ergonomic for a leg sleeve. I made a pair of boxer-briefs, so the power wire stays short." He looked at me. "They've been tested, so you may want to wash them."

"Thanks for the heads up. How long until it learns my walk?" I limped over to the stairs. I had to find a chair and switch these wraps from my hands to my calf. I looked around and noticed the audience had lost interest and returned to their workouts.

Ace tuned out, as if studying equations on a spectral grease board. He blinked and caught up to me. "An hour and forty minutes."

I smiled at him, *Excellent.*

* * *

"Oh my God. That's not true," Blondie disagreed in a high tone.

"Yes it is," Shocker insisted. She squirmed in the front passenger seat of the Scion, shooting frowns at the driver. Ace kept his eyes on the road and his smile to himself.

Blondie and I enjoyed the snug comfort of the tiny back seat. Or rather, I did. She couldn't run from me. The bombshell almost absently noticed my hand sneaking up her leg and pinched it to a halt, right as my fingers felt the heat coming of her blonde pubbies. She grabbed the perverted hand, replaced it on her knee, not even bothering herself with a glare for me. She was completely absorbed with debating her friend. "If three minute rounds are so much better, how come most female fighters still train and fight for two minutes?" she wanted to know.

Shocker twisted around, exasperated that someone would challenge her authority on the subject. "Because it would be more work for the same amount of money."

"What???" My girl looked beyond cute when puzzled. I made her go through the sneak-pinch-replace hand thing again.

"If you had experienced promoters in the pros you'd know what I mean. Those guys suck. A promoter will not pay a girl more for a fight just because it has three minute rounds. Starting out, girls get two hundred dollars a round. A two minute round. If all of a sudden rounds were changed to three minutes, promoters are not going to offer three hundred a round. That's not going to happen."

Blondie folded her arms, frowning. "So doesn't that support the argument for two minute rounds?"

Shocker let out a breath. Her passion for the subject was showing, an old wellspring of emotion that hasn't been tapped like this in a very long time. She put on a patient, experienced professor air. "No. The whole system needs to be revamped. I wish you could talk to some of the girls I know. In two thousand and six Layla McCarter was the first woman to have a title fight with three minute rounds."

"She fought Belinda Laracuente," Blondie said.

"Mmm-hmm."

"I thought you were the first," I said.

Shocker twisted again and gave me a curious glance. "Didn't figure you for a reader."

I responded with a certain finger stuck up in front of an appropriate scowl.

She smiled, *Kidding*. "I was one of the first." She looked at my girl. "In two thousand and seven Layla fought Donna Biggers in Vegas in the first women's bout scheduled for twelve three minute rounds. She is the pioneer. I jumped on the bandwagon because it was a chance to stick it to the promoters and get some girls on TV with bigger paydays."

"What's the real advantage to three minutes versus two?" I said. "More time to set up shots?"

She nodded. Ace cursed traffic that surrounded us. It was just past sundown, sky dark overhead but brilliant with blues, greens and oranges to our right, colors brighter along the horizon lining the black Gulf. The confusing array of lights produced by rush hour traffic winked and glowed among numerous engines, rolling tires and occasional horn or booming stereo. Exhaust fumes seeped in through the cracked windows.

Shocker smiled at Ace's reference to burnt electronics, then looked back at us. "In two minutes it's hard to show off your skill as a boxer. You basically have to get out there and throw a bunch of punches to get points or a stoppage. Like in the amateurs. With three minutes women can show that they have skills equal to men." She looked pointedly at me. "Or better..."

"Pfff," I replied, making the girls chortle.

Shocker went on. "Two minute rounds disrupt the flow of fights. Trust me. When you get into a rhythm for three minute rounds you feel more like a pro."

"But fewer and shorter rounds limit wear and tear on boxers, allowing us to fight more frequently." Blondie rebutted. "And two minutes is a faster pace. Makes the fights more exciting."

"That's a good argument, one many women are making," Shocker acquiesced. "But it won't give us equal rights in the sport, or allow pure boxers the chance to get recognized. If we had true equality, maybe we'd have the opportunity to fight on HBO or Showtime and make half the cash men generate."

Blondie nodded thoughtfully. I said, "Babe, cash wins any debate. Shocker: four. Blondie: three." Ace chuckled with me until we were glared into silence.

Blondie's leg tensed under my hand. In a disturbingly quiet tone she asked me, "So you guys are keeping score on us?"

I looked into her gorgeous yes with a shit-eating grin. "Yes we are."

"I, uh..." Ace muttered.

Shocker stared out the windshield and told her man, "Well then, you won't be keeping any scores when we get home tonight."

Ace looked at me in the rear view mirror. It's possible I encouraged him with an Are You going To Take That? look. He glanced right and retorted, "That's okay. I have a new girlfriend on *World of Warcraft*."

"I hope she's hot," Shocker said. I could see her profile, lips trying to pucker back a grin. His attempts at humor would apparently disarm any trouble with his wife.

"She's a troll," he said in his matter-of-fact manner.

I offered, "I'd hit that."

Blondie smacked me. Shocker decided it was a good idea and smacked Ace. We rubbed our arms and grinned at our women, excited about wining our first Guys Vs. Girls match up. They grinned back, no doubt thinking they had won.

We turned off the highway, then onto Oak Street, cruising into the heart of Biloxi's east end. We arrived at our destination seconds later. The Buddhist temple was an unlikely evening spot for four young Caucasians, but we had an It's Cool pass because we were invited to a celebration here by *Anh Long*. And I mean a real celebration. The Autumn Festival is serious business to the Vietnamese. They went all out, with festive decorations and colorful dress, tables full of food, dancing. Contests. It was a huge family event, the "family" part having been stressed to me by both Blondie and Shocker, for whatever reason. I didn't care. I was attending to try my hand at dragon dancing. I had no exact idea what that entailed but it sounded like something I should have been doing all my life.

The boring-ass church next door needs to take note: the temple knows how to make religion fun.

The temple grounds were fenced in, front gate open in two places for driveways. Ace turned into the first one, piloting us through rows of cars in the parking area. It was packed. I noticed the vehicles were nearly all imports, in factory condition. The crowd would be mostly conservative Vietnamese, parents and grandparents, working-class folks and maybe a few retired gangsters. Lots of kids. *Damn. Kids. Blondie will be oohing and ahing all night.* Where the hell is Big Guns? We were supposed to meet up and burn one before making our entrance.

Ace found a space next to the only customized ride in the lot, a red Mitsubishi Evo. I looked the ride over, analytically, hoping its passengers would be cool enough to party with until Big Guns showed.

The driver is probably a fifteen year old dealer from the Royal Family, my ever-optimistic subconscious opined, jacked up on a fresh dose of Dexadrine. *Ten to one he's one of the dragon dancers.*

Ace shifted into PARK and killed the ignition. He and Shocker opened the doors, warm fresh air rushing past the front seats as they adjusted them so we could climb out. I watched my girl go first, lending a gentlemanly hand where I thought appropriate. She squealed and threatened me, squirmed away from my groping and stood on the pavement. Shook out her long locks. The parking lot lights made her snug fitting jacket shine expensively, crimson hide that looked nearly black. Her designer jeans were black and tight, showing off hell-fuck-yeah legs, long black-crimson boots ending just below her knees, heels knocking with authority. She took some things out of a scarlet handbag and pocketed them, tossed the bag in the back seat and closed the door. Looked around in a circle. "Where's Big G?"

I climbed out behind Ace. "Maybe he rode with someone else?" I speculated.

She shrugged, *Oh well.*

Ace closed the door, then checked out his girl while he played with his blonde spikes, getting them just right. His thermal blue long sleeve utility shirt went perfectly with the hybrid skinny jeans/cargo pants. Very techno nerd. He had gadgets of unknown design on his belt and leg pockets, arm pockets. A yellow light blinked next to his knee. Polished metal flashed at his waist and thighs.

What the fuck???

I looked over at Shocker. At first I had been surprised she wore the compression sleeve to this function. But after seeing Ace's ensemble I decided she had been extorted into going along with a cyborg geek couples matching scheme. She looked over the roof at him, scratching her bionic arm. She wore a different, far more stylish Power Felt top. It was white with one gray long sleeve, thick black stitching, the left sleeve missing. The silky, scale-like compression sleeve filled its place. There was a gap between the top and sleeve, wires and tan skin visible. Her shorts were mid-thigh, white, cargo pockets on each muscular leg fully utilized: they contained her brass knuckles. She patted her pockets absently, reassuring herself, a good mechanic never leaving home without her tools.

Shocker's hiking boots were white and gray, brushed leather, tall enough to emphasize calves that didn't need any help. Her over-developed gastrocs made a plain enough statement without accessorizing. *I can beat you – and YOU – at anything,* the freaky gorgeous things proclaimed loudly.

As long as Ace stands next to her no one will make fun of him, I predicted.

She noticed my look and gestured at herself. "Yeah it was his turn to win." She shrugged. "It was either this or help him build a giant lantern that hovers." She straightened her back and deepened her voice, mimicking her husband's one squinted eye. *"The Autumn Festival is also called the Lantern Festival."*

"Not bad," I said.

"Yeah. Lantern festival," Ace said, completely missing the sarcasm. "Part of the celebration is a lighting of lanterns. They have a contest and write riddles on the paper lanterns." He looked around at us. "You guys want to hear mine?"

I showed him an eager face and invited, "Tell me less."

Blondie cut her eyes at me in disapproval, then looked at the geek. "Did you Google the Autumn Festival?"

"Binged it," he replied. "What? You guys didn't?"

I turned my back to him and fought for control of my face.

Blondie told him, "We aren't on a job, honey." She took a compact and tube of lipstick from her front pocket. Opened both. I could see her plump pink lips in the compact's mirror as she swiped on a quick touch up. "Besides, if we needed to know something about this party or the people here I wouldn't have to research it." She pocketed her makeup.

"Yeah, there's plenty of old Viet players here that are going to hit on you," I said. "They'll tell you all you want to know about the Autumn Fest. And their Sausage Fest."

"Ew! If any old player fests his sausage anywhere near me, I'll use his ass like a gong." She smacked a fist into her palm, mugging me fiercely for putting such an unpleasant image in her head. "Fucker." She pushed me.

"Hey. If you get disgusted, just think of this." I waved my hands down my sides, chest out arrogantly. Put my palms together above my head and wagged my face side to side while squatting and hopping, beat-boxing a Bollywood jam. The girls burst out laughing, watching my ridiculous antics.

My pants were black leather, though thin and worn enough to look like jeans. I wore a dark red thermal tee, tucked in, belt buckle plasma sculpted into a miniature straight razor. It was chrome, opened slightly. Because it will be cold later I wore a white leather 'cycle jacket with red stripes down the sleeves, unzipped. No jewelry. My hair and 'stache were gleaming. My Johnson was scheming. We were ready for our entrance.

My bitch is badder than yours, my proud smile told the two men that walked past the Scion, forty-ish Viet locals that couldn't take their eyes off the girls. Their heads twisted around comically, legs still marching straight, captivated by Blondie's butt and Shocker's tan, ripped legs. We began walking behind them. They faced front, laughing about something. The girls' curves bulged and flexed in ways their tiny Asian women never could. I wasn't offended by their leering. Hey, I understood.

I've driven by this place for years but never thought I'd have a reason to be here. The temple was at the rear of the property, an almost Spanish-style building of white stucco with a red tile roof. Its facade was pleasing in design, open archways rather than columns. A tall white stone statue was on a pedestal in front of it, an Asian chick in a robe.

Compassionate Mother, my subconscious provided.

How the hell did I know that? The amount of useless information in my head could fill the Library of Congress.

Next to the temple was a modular home with white vinyl siding and a shingled roof, a gray KIA parked in front. Likely the residence of the caretaker. Neither of those buildings were important at the moment, however. The party was at the pavilion out front.

Over a hundred people thronged the archways, red brick walls and cement patios around the stylish pavilion. Its roof was a match to the temple, red tile with corners swooping out and curving up at the tips, an architectural mix of modern and old school oriental. CHUA VAN DUC was on the top of the center archway in large red letters, BUDDHIST TEMPLE under it. Temple of a million fortunes, I think it translated to. Flags flapped on top of the swooped roof: the U.S. flag, the Vietnam flag, and one I didn't recognize. Grass, flower beds, and assorted plants were landscaped around it, colorful lights strung over tables with food and drinks, bright red glares fogging my vision. Most of the people were dressed casually, though some wore nice suits and traditional robes. Everyone wore a smile, and spoke in Vietnamese.

The Elder Dragon stood among several men and women, all of them in robes. The men's garb was golden yellow or orange-gold, the ladies pale blue and pale gray. *Anh Long* looked like a king visiting his subjects. He moved slowly, speaking with everyone, eye contact timed perfectly, grasping hands and bowing affectionately. I could see why he was so revered. The man had serious charisma.

For the most part the crowd welcomed us with polite hellos, though a few older women frowned up severely when they saw Blondie and Shocker. We were certainly out of place. I was taking a perverse pride in making the conservatives uncomfortable when *Anh Long* walked over and shook our hands.

"Welcome. I'm so happy you could make it," he said, looking at each of us. His epicanthic eyes shined behind his glasses, smile genuine and comfortable on his ageless face.

"I'm here for the dragon dancing," I told him, then inclined my head at my crew. "They're here for the spiritual crap."

"I see," he replied, humor brightening his eyes even more. "Do you know the purpose of the spiritual crap?"

"Of course," I said in mock offense. "It's a reason to throw a party."

"*Hmmpt*," Blondie agreed.

"Like you need a reason to throw a party," Shocker told me.

"I don't." I pointed at her, very serious. I gave my voice a solemn tone. "But you do. I'm here to help you people embrace your inner party animal." I took a deep breath, let it out. "It's a higher level of Zen."

Blondie rolled her eyes. Ace grinned. Shocker looked piqued by my Zen comment. *Anh Long* put a hand on my shoulder and returned my solemnity. "And we are thankful for your help. Please feel free to show us how to achieve this higher level."

"You might want to rethink that, sir," Blondie said, very concerned. "Your congregation might lose its religion after a night of him capering around here."

The Elder Dragon just smiled. "I trust him to mind his manners around the children present and respect our beliefs."

Damn. I scowled at Blondie, at him. He basically said he trusted me. I hate it when people do that. Now I had to be all PG-13 and shit. "Great," I muttered.

Blondie and *Anh Long* shared a knowing look. She gave him a thumbs up. He returned the gesture, then took Shocker aside. "Do you remember Cung Le?" he asked her.

"The kick boxer?" she said. "Yeah. Bad boy. He's in MMA now." He nodded, then pointed to the Vietnam flag on top of the pavilion. Her eyes widened. She said, "Oh yeah! Cung wears that on his trunks."

His face showed excited passion. "The three red stripes stand for North, Central, and South Vietnam…"

I turned at the sound of loud laughter. A group of young girls in white, gray and red silk dresses were really chatting it up, huddled around a phone that must be playing some kind of OMG-LOL video. Girlie giggle-talking in Vietnamese was not something I saw every day. It sounded pretty cool. The frustrated frowns of the women standing behind them said it wasn't special for very long.

"I need a drink," I decided, smacking my lips.

"You can't," Ace said loudly, so I could hear him over all the fun. I just looked at him. Blondie smirked, *Whatever* and walked over to look at the food. Ace watched her go, looked back at me and shrugged. "Well, you're not supposed to. No alcohol on temple grounds. It's sacrilegious."

"I guess I should have binged it, huh? We are drinking," I pointed at him, a thumb at myself, "and then we're taking over that dragon. It is written, and so it shall be."

"Uh," he replied.

I motioned for him to follow me. We tried not to look like we were headed anywhere in particular, so when we bumped into the old gangster it looked as if by chance. Hong looked ancient in a dark green long sleeve shirt and black tie, bald pate dark brown with gray fringe over hairy ears and a chubby face. A disturbing, toothless smile. I met Hong when I was fourteen. He sold crack on the Point, and I supplied him with transportation. Mostly. We learned a little of each other's language and made a bunch of cash. *I was a dirt bike ninja in those days*, I recalled with pride.

"My friend, my friend!" Hong said in nearly incomprehensible English, rheumy eyes alight with social cheer and quality alcohol. "*May kheo khong?*" how are you?

"*Tao kheo*," I'm good, I replied, gripping his strong stubby hand. I leaned in and spoke quietly next to his ear. "Where's the booze, you damn thug? There's no way I'm going to enjoy this party sober."

"Oh, ha-ha! Come. We talk." He said something to his friends, two distinguished men in suits with evening-dressed ladies on their arms, and excused himself. He turned and noticed Ace, features turning comical as he squinted at the geek. "Who this?" he demanded to know.

"Julian," Ace said, holding out his hand.

Hong looked down at it, up at his face. Squinted again. He gave an impatient bow, jerked his head at me and we followed the squat old man through the crowd and into the parking lot. We stopped at a neat looking maroon and silver Acura RDX. Hong opened the crossover's back hatch, hydraulic shock hissing. The cargo area had a black cover with a small window in the center in the shape of a money sign. Hong pushed a toggle switch next to the cover's latch and money green light glowed through the window, glass fogged with cold condensation. He hit a second toggle and the latch popped open, cooler whining open softly, clicking to a stop fully open. An alcoholic's Holy Grail confronted us. Bottles of liquor were separated from bottles of wine, some with ice, some encased in insulation, dry. Tall bottles of Heineken and Michelob glistened from sections of ice water. The green light glowed from beneath each clear bottomed section, making the colorful glass refract like dazzling treasure. A small section on the right side had slots for utensils. Several styles of bottle openers winked sharply in the shadowed interior light.

I knuckled Ace on the shoulder. "Blondie built this."

"Yeah?" He leaned over and inspected the materials closely. "Hmm. Simple fiberglass and Lexan job. Elegant. The money sign is a nice touch." He stood and I grabbed us some beers.

"Uh-uh." Hong grabbed my wrist. "My friend, we have special drink. Here." He leaned into the vehicle and grabbed a bottle of red wine, turned it and studied the label. "Ah! This the one."

"What is it?" Ace said.

Hong was silent for a moment, then scowled at him. "I don't know. I can't read English."

I peered at the bottle. "It's French."

He turned his scowl on me, squinting ferociously. Waved a hand wildly. "You want drink, or no? This the one."

"I want drink," I said.

Ace was still inspecting my girl's work. "Why a cooler?" he asked Hong.

He showed his disturbing gummy smile. "Some people like speaker in box." He grabbed a cork screw and opened the wine, grunting. *Thwump!* The strong scent of quality Merlot attacked my nose. Hong sniffed the cork. "I like booze in box."

The alcohol mercenary handed me the wine and leaned back into his booze box, grabbing several Gatorade bottles from a section with beverages for mixing drinks. Soda, water, juice. He handed each of us a 32 oz. jug and took the wine back. We cracked the tops and poured them out on the ground.

"Are you idiots having a peeing contest?" Blondie said from behind us.

I turned and pretended to zip up my pants. "Nope."

She looked at the flood on the pavement, eyebrows raised. "That's a shitload of pee. Hey Hong." She smiled at him.

"Uh," Ace said.

"Blondie! My friend." Hong cried happily, waving his bottle at her. "Join us." He hit my arm and accused me, "Why you not bring your lady for drink?"

I held up a finger. "First, let me clarify something: she's no lady." Now Blondie hit me in the arm. "And she wasn't invited because she's going to nag me for drinking tonight."

"*She's going to nag me for drinking tonight,*" she mimicked. Ace and Hong laughed for some reason. My hand twitched, wanting to twist her nipple. She put a hand on her hip, tight jacket creaking around her shoulders. "You guys do whatever you like. But," she pointed at me, "if you expose these kids to anything…"

"Yeah, yeah. Got it." *Geez. Always kids with her lately. Kids kids kids. She finds a way to bring them up every day now.*

With one last meaningful look for me, she spun on a toe and strutted back to the party. Hong and I watched her, booze momentarily forgotten. Ace tried hard not to look.

With our jugs full of vintage Merlot, I held mine up for a toast. "To the Autumn Festival! Come on grape Gatorade. Make the women look hotter and the children more tolerable."

"*Do!*" cheers, Hong barked.

"Cheers," Ace said. We touched jugs and drank, then Ace said, "Grape Gatorade. Hah."

We made our way back to the crowd, sipping happily, and stopped at a procession of people picking over a table of food. Community volunteers stood on the other side, serving soft drinks and rice cakes, a tasty selection of candied and dried fruit, and what looked like tofu something-or-other. "Eh. Vegan food." I shuddered.

Hong nodded brisk agreement. "Men should eat animal." He flexed his bicep, then grabbed mine. "No animal, no man."

"You hear that, Ace?" I said.

"I eat meat," he said defensively, looking down at his lanky body. He looked at me with smug, squinted, secret knowledge. He tapped his temple. "It's just that my brain requires much more than the rest of me."

"Hmm," I replied. He was attempting to joke but was likely telling it right. *Dude is scary smart,* my subconscious agreed.

Hong looked at him askance. He pointed to a cake on the table to our right. "I bring that. Wife make it. Very good, you try?"

"Who the hell would marry you?" I asked. Hung gave me a raspy chuckle, moving his lips and tongue in a way to let us know how he scored a wife. His epicanthic eyes rounded, shining with spirit. I shook my head, set my jug on the table. I selected a small slice of the cake with a napkin, took a bite. "It's good," I said, forcing myself to swallow. The speed had taken my appetite and saliva. This cake didn't bring it back.

Ace looked at me, at the cake. "Hmm."

"Mung bean cake," Hong told us. "Traditional. Like Christmas fruit cake."

I traded the cake for my bottle and drank deeply. *Mung bean cake???* I looked around, sensing the crowd hush for a presentation. Next to the pavilion a small stage had been erected. On the platform six young girls in silk dresses were formed up in a line, small wooden handled fans held up next to their cheeks, waiting for music to start. An older woman in a faded gray robe, presumably the girls' instructor, pushed play on a boom box and grinned matronly pride as a stringed oriental song began to jam.

The little girls smiled cutely, red, gray and blue silk glimmering in the lights. They moved in sync, holding fans high, then low, fluttering them up next to their cheeks again. They turned in a circle, wood and paper flapping, executing simple movements that would be boring to watch if the dancers weren't so adorable. *Whoa whoa whoa! Adorable??? I'm glad you didn't say that out loud,* my subconscious laughed. *You scored a gay-and-lame twofer with that one, pal.*

Cheers and clapping erupted from several men as Blondie and Shocker stepped up on the stage, fans in hand, and joined the dance. I noticed several highly reserved ladies shooting evil looks at them and the leering men. A smile I felt would become indefinite assaulted my facial muscles. The tiny girls giggled as Shocker messed up, turning the wrong way. She laughed at herself, shrugged her muscled shoulders.

The dance went on for another few minutes, ending with the song. Applause followed the performance, the kids on stage ecstatic, Blondie and Shocker high-fiving them. They all walked off the platform and the audience turned their attention back to the food tables or whatever group they had been socializing with.

My bottle dripped empty over my extended tongue. I capped it, planning to refill it shortly. The Merlot was spectacular, a perfect counter to the amphetamines still juicing my system. A comfortable warmth had taken over my limbs, expelling the pain still trying to emanate from under the compression legging covering my lower left leg. The wine was thick on my breath, saturating. The aftertaste made me feel like dancing. I turned to Ace. "It's time."

"For what?" he replied.

"To dance. Come on, let's find Big Guns. We need three people."

"How do you know we need three?"

Ace wasn't completely down with my plan, but he followed me anyway, studying something on the screen of a tablet he had taken from his pocket. We found the Asian goon standing with his crew near the parking area. The Royal Family, a subset of the Dragon Family, were mostly seasoned gangsters that owned businesses and young traffickers hoping to follow in their footsteps. This particular clique, Big Guns' lieutenants and personal security, consisted of older members. Mature, well dressed men that were past the juvenile, pants sagging stage of their gang careers. I recognized a few of them, nodding *What's up* as we approached. I bumped into their leader's back a little too hard and growled, "Watch where you're going, little yellow man."

Big Guns spun around ready for confrontation, hand at his waist, the other balled up. His mouth turned down with silver irritation. "One of these days I'll shoot you for that."

I pointed at my face and showed all my teeth. My canines felt like daggers. "You see I'm worried."

"Ace," he said to the geek, bumping fists, ignoring my efforts to look terrified. "How long have you guys been here?"

"A couple hours," Ace said. He held up his Gatorade bottle. "Though the time has been flying." He took a drink.

Big Guns shook his head and smiled. His short muscular arms bulged in his black and silver shirt, jet hair styled with a part on the side, shining with class. He looked at me. "Hong?" I shrugged, *No idea what you mean, mon.* He said, "*Anh Long* will sacrifice him to Buddha if he finds out."

"I thought we were supposed to smoke one then dragon dance," I complained, wanting to do something with this buzz before it wore off.

He looked around at his crew, appearing to search their waists. His scan stopped on a child's head peeking between the legs of two burly gangsters. "Tho! *Lai day*," come here, Big Guns said sternly.

Tho's tiny, sharp cheeks rounded, smile showing several adult teeth growing in. He squirmed through the men and stopped in front of his *Anh Hai*, looking much better dressed than when I last saw him in his cock fighting clothes. His jeans and Saints jersey set him apart from the other kids present, who wore dressier attire. I liked that. I had a feeling this dude would throw a serious tantrum if someone tried to make him wear such nice clothing. The swag he affected in front of the Royal Family was impressive. He was a different kid than the humble servant that tended *Anh Long's* rooster. "What?" he said roughly, covering a high pitch.

Big Guns looked the boy over, shaking his head, as if reminded of someone. "Were you planning on dancing tonight? You should be practicing with Dong and Tran."

Tho folded his arms. "I'm just a stupid tail. The dragon dance is stupid." He dropped his head. Scrubbed a sneaker over the pavement.

Chrome exasperation flashed between Big Guns' lips. I gave him a raised brow, *Give me a shot at it?* He grunted, *Why not?* and I waved a hand in front of the kid's face. "Hey little man." He looked at me, not in the least shy, a cocky, intelligent little motherfucker. "So you think dragon dancing is lame, huh?"

"It's stupid. It's not even *fun*." He folded his arms tight and frowned emphatically.

I leaned down and said in a confidential tone, "Have you ever heard of the Godzilla dance?"

Tho's mouth parted slightly, eyes huge with wonder. "Godzilla is a kind of like a dragon," he said.

I nodded seriously. "Except Godzilla knows how to have more fun. He doesn't just fly around and look friendly, expecting everyone to feel fortuitous – he smashes stuff and sets things on fire!"

"Really? Whoa!" Tho exclaimed. "Can we do that? Where does Godzilla come from?"

"You know the guys that made PlayStation?"

"Sony."

"Yeah, those guys. So you know he's cool."

Big Guns gave me an odd look. *Where are you going with this?*

I held a finger up to him and said to Tho, "Are you qualified to play Godzilla?"

The boy started thinking hard, desperately wanting to claim he was worthy. His eyes widened suddenly and he blurted, "One time I played *Mario Kart* as Yoshi. Yoshi is kind of like Godzilla."

I clapped my hands once, sharply. "You're in!" He showed everyone his snaggle-tooth grin, skinny arms gesturing excitedly.

Big Guns snorted at me. He looked at Tho. "*Em Chai*, you have to ask permission to dance the dragon. Didn't you already tell Miss Nguyen you didn't want to do it? You know how she is about people that can't make up their mind."

Tho's cocky smile vanished. He turned to look at a group of older women in robes, eyes resentful. I followed his eyes to the lady that had instructed the girls' fan dance earlier, surmising she was Miss Nguyen. She looked intimidating. I could see why Tho quit with the swag.

Pep talk, my subconscious suggested.

I squatted down in front of Tho, eye-to-eye. "Look kid. If you want to be Godzilla, you can't be afraid of old ladies."

He glanced at Miss Nguyen, then whispered to me, "But she's crazy."

Snickers from the Royal Family made Tho scowl. I just barely kept the smile from my face. I told the boy, "You can out-think crazy," I tapped a finger on his forehead, "with this." He gave me a quizzical look. The wine and amphetamines decided I needed to give this young prospect a lesson on working people. I took a breath and explained the ABCs of Approach. "Forget about how crazy she is. You just have to know how to approach her."

"How?" He stuck his hands out, palms up.

"Whenever you want something big from someone, you have to get them to agree to something small first." I paused for him to consider that. He nodded. I continued, "For example, if you wanted your uncle

Big Guns to buy you a new video game, talk to him about something that interests *him* first."

"Like guns," Tho said immediately. "I'm gonna be Royal Fam' too." He put a hand on his chest and nodded importantly. Everyone chuckled.

"Like guns," I agreed, then noticed Blondie and Shocker were standing behind me, their perfume alerting. I glanced at them and saw Ace and Bobby, as well as an immense black lady who must be Mrs. Big Swoll, standing next to them. Two young girls in eyelet dresses, her daughters, stood a few feet behind her, watching the adults. I pretended the women weren't looking at me as if catching me doing something wrong. "Water guns. Exactly. If you know Uncle Big Guns likes Super Soakers, you can say you like them so he'll agree with you. You could talk about his car. Tell him you like his Honda better than that Toyota." I pointed at a white Supra. "His attitude will become agreeable."

"Then I ask him for a new game?"

"Yep."

He looked thoughtful. Looked up at Big Guns. "I'm gonna make you buy me the new *Halo!*"

Big Guns snorted doubtfully. His crew snickered again.

I told Tho, "And you're a kid. So use that too."

"How?" Palms up.

I wiggled my fingers in front of his face. "Touch. Touching someone, if done right, strengthens relationships, and is a marker of closeness we recognize instinctively. Squeeze a shoulder, rub a forearm, and you trigger a process."

"Huh?"

"Here's how it works: When you stimulate pressure receptors in the skin, you lower stress hormones." At this point I realized I had completely lost the kid. He was back to scowling at the Royal Family for laughing at him. I also realized I was too high to stop myself. "At the same time, warm touch stimulates the release of oxytocin, which enhances a sense of trust and attachment."

"Oxy..." he stumbled.

"Tocin. Uh."

"The cuddle hormone," Ace provided. "You can experience it in many situations. Like at a barber shop. A barber touches your scalp and neck and it feels good. A good hug from someone who loves you will do it every time."

I grinned at him, *Thanks*. Tho's eyes widened. He understood the power of cuddling, apparently. He told me, "That must be how Trinh got a new car!"

The RF burst out laughing. So did the girls, after Blondie told them Trinh was Big Guns' girlfriend. The Viet leader shot her a promising stare. He shook a finger at Tho and spouted off rapid Vietnamese that made the boy take off running, smile plastered to his face.

"So, you're teaching kids the psychology of influence now?" Blondie asked, linking her long wicked arm through mine as I stood. "I guess I should expect more of that when we have kids."

"I don't know what you're talking about," I replied in perfect inno-cence. "I'm just trying to dance. Need to test drive this new leg." *When we have kids???* She gave me her Yeah Right smirk.

"You must be Razor," Bobby's girl said, voice strong, tone hinting that I better not deny my identity. Her dark brown face was without makeup, pretty as a plus-size model, eye lashes and short black hair artificial but complimentary. She put a hand on her hip. Looked me over from feet to head. "You don't look like no hero."

I glanced at Big Swoll and gestured, *What the hell, man?* He wore a secret smile, proud of his wife's ability to make me uncomfortable. The giant looked resplendent in a colorful button-up, purples and blues that contrasted with the bright floral print on his wife's dress. She was nearly as tall as he was, at least six-three, two forty, well-proportioned in spite of the weight six daughters had given her.

I glanced at Blondie's hips and flat stomach, back to her. *Nope. Uh-uh*. Laughter made me look toward the food tables. Their four other daughters were running around playing tag with the Vietnamese kids, wired on Kool-Aid and candy.

"I'm Pearl," Big Swollette said, thrusting a strong hand at me. I shook it, still pondering her hero remark.

"He's pleased to meet you," Blondie said, taking over, shaking her head at me.

The women started gabbing about something or other. I waved at Ace. My eyes told him, *Perfect. Let's make our escape.* The geek followed me through the RF members and then through the crowd under the pavilion. We approached the group of robed women surrounding Tho, stopping just in earshot, pretending we were checking out decorations lining the pavilion's roof. They weren't speaking in English.

Ace said, "Can you understand what they're saying?"

The Dexedrine driving my cognitive functions allows me to comprehend ANYTHING. I listened for a moment. "Shortround just commented on a skirt. No, a dress." We watched the kid. He had all the ladies smiling, pulling at their robes and making pleased sounds. "Robes. They are agreeing about the color being nice."

"Tho learns fast," Ace said.

Shortround carried on for several sentences, saying something about dancing in a robe. He bent his legs and arms, springing them in all directions as he danced around. The women cackled laughter. The rascal spun around and stopped in front of Miss Nguyen, grabbing her shoulder. He gently squeezed it while telling her she made him feel like dancing again, he was sorry about changing his mind, and could he use the dragon to dance with two *my trang*, white boys?

Unable to stop laughing, she patted his cheek, pleased with his good behavior; he made her look good in front of her friends. She gave him consent to dance with his friends and he took off so fast I swear he produced Road Runner sound effects. *Meep-Meep! Bvvv-vooomm!*

"I'm hallucinating," I chuckled. "Excellent." I motioned to Ace. "Finally.Let's get funky."

"I can't dance," he replied, frowning. "And the dragon only needs two people." He patted his holstered tablet.

"It's more like playing. Just have fun. Tho and I will handle the showmanship." I waved off his excuse. "The more people we have the better. 'Zilla's grown a couple extra legs since he attacked New York."

We walked toward the temple. Under the center archway was the dragon. It lay on the cement, already assembled, about nine feet long and three feet wide, red and yellow with a little blue and purple in the face. A traditional dragon with a wide smiling mouth and long whiskers protruding from his muzzle. The mouth was wide open, two big canines up top, two on the bottom jaw. Tho knelt next to the bamboo and papier-mâché contraption, small hands fumbling with handles on the side. I told him, "Wait wait wait. I get to be the head, kid. You're the tail."

He looked like he wanted to spit. "The tail is stupid."

I held up a hand, "No, the *dragon* tail is stupid." I pointed at the colorful beast. "This is Godzilla. And Godzilla's tail smashes stuff."

"Oh," he said, standing, walking to the tail with a mischievous smile, "*Godzilla's* tail"

Ace chuckled. "You'd make a great dad."

I took offense. "How would you know?"

"I have a son and a daughter," he replied slowly, eyeing me uncertainly.

"Hmm." That inconvenient exchange made me look down at the Gatorade bottles still in our hands. Mine was empty, his half full. I sat mine on the concrete and pointed at his. "You going to finish that?"

"Well, I –"

"Gimme." I swiped it from his grasp, twisted off the cap and turned that baby up like a wino, draining the Merlot with deep chugs. *Challenge*, the alcohol said to the amphetamines. I dropped the bottle, plastic clattering, and burped loudly. I sensed numerous eyes turn in my direction. I smacked my lips, savoring the aftertaste. "Good sipping wine. You ready?" I looked at Ace. "You get to be the belly. Guts, organs, penis and shit."

I leaned over and grabbed the dragon's head, looked into its human-like eyes. "It's show time, Godzilla. Let's show these nice folks how dragons party. Sony-style."

"Yeah!" Tho agreed. "We'll play like in a video game!"

Bright kid. I smiled. We lifted the prop and ducked under it. Its frame was square bamboo ribs, assembled so the dragon could bend in several directions. It had no discernible smell other than a fresh coat of paint on the face.

I stood up straight, lifting it, holding onto handles in front of my chest that allowed me to maneuver the head and open/close the mouth. I shook Godzilla's head, a disgruntled, drunken beast that had been wronged by all the other Asian dragons, and felt the need to prove himself right in the eyes of the people. Show that he was the best at making people feel auspicious.

"RAAAHRRR!" Godzilla bellowed. "'Zilla stomp and hump!"

"Stump and hump!" the tailed echoed, wagging. Ace's chuckle rang hollowly from the belly.

"Rah?" Big Guns said walking over to us, two of his boys walking close behind, eyes searching all directions. "You sound like you need more wine."

"Or something, right? Where's Blondie?" I peered out the wide mouth, searching for the only golden hairdo present, thinking about her boobies and the baggie of Dexedrine tucked in next to them.

He grunted, *I don't keep up with your girl,* then stepped closer and pointed his chin at a guy standing far off to the side of the pavilion, next to the fence separating the temple from the church. I squinted, trying to make out who the person in black was. His statue-still, be-the-shadow posture told me. "Loc," I said in wonder. I looked at Big Guns. "What the hell?"

He grunted. "Remember what I told you about his girl getting jumped by the Two-Eleven?"

"She was pregnant. She lost the baby because of the injuries and left him."

Grunt. "It happened on this night ten years ago." His voice added a little melodrama. "Vietnamese are superstitious about dead loved ones. We honor them on the anniversary of their deaths."

"Does *Anh Long* know he's here?"

He grunted affirmative. "We pretend he isn't for his comfort. *Thang Loc Khun dien*," Loc is crazy. He showed his silver grill. "We honor that too."

I shook Godzilla's head, growling. "Well, honor these 'Zilla nuts, little yellow man. We're about to get crazy."

"Crazy Godzilla nuts!" Tho shouted, whipping the tail back and forth.

Ace laughed. "I thought I was the nuts."

"Let the kid swing 'em," I said. I gripped the handles and Big Guns stepped back quickly, wanting no part of 'Zilla's devious intentions.

Ace and Tho were on point. We trotted over to the pavilion as one six-legged organism. The Elder Dragon spotted us and gestured at groups of robed men and women to watch our dance, speaking loudly in Vietnamese. *This is the man*, he told them.

Peering from under Godzilla's upper teeth I recognized several of the onlookers as D'Iberville business owners, ones who had been extorted by the Two-Eleven and OBG. The restaurant owners we had helped were front and center, pointing and smiling at me, telling their friends in boisterous sing-song tones about my crew taking out the enemy and returning their daughter's costume jewelry.

I paused, uncomfortable, Ace stumbling behind me. I noticed the conservative mugs in the congregation were looking at me with more favorable expressions now, and I didn't like it.

No! Don't do that my subconscious wailed. *Look at me like I'm a Bad Guy. A barbarian. I* swear *I'm bad. I can't take any more affection!*

"Godzilla's tail!" Tho shouted in a high-pitched war cry, running over and crashing into a table of food. The perfectly executed tail slash toppled several two-liter bottles of soda, plastic bouncing, rolling under the tables. Surprised squawks resounded among the women, and I eagerly soaked up their disapproval, feeling the spirit again.

"Tho!" I laughed. "Not the tables, dude. The trash cans. Smash the trash cans."

"Okay," he agreed happily, jumping up and down, psyched, looking left, right, for a trash barrel.

I hopped up and down to match the kid's rhythm, 'Zilla's belly stationary as the head and tail undulated, serpentine. Laughter and clapping started, people beginning to cheer us on. Miss Nguyen DJed for us, her little boom box coming to life with a fast tempoed song, drums rumbling, stringed chords thrumming an Asian jam. A melodic chanting began from the fan dance girls, Miss Nguyen and her associates taking it up seconds later. All the ingredients were in place. It was time to Entertain.

"Waaaah!" I screamed. "I am the Kung-Fu Master." My lips moved out of sync with my words. "You will never defeat me!"

"Waaaah!" Tho aped, giddy.

I stepped around quickly, throwing short, explosive front kicks, to my left, right, front, bobbing and shaking the massive head after every one. Ace and Tho did their best to mimic my moves, feeling the energy. The crowd loved it.

"Hey kid," I spun around to look at my tail. "You believe in Buddhism, right? Reincarnation?" I kept kicking, bobbing and shaking.

"Yeah," he said, kicking his skinny legs quickly.

I began stomping and jumping as if my boots hit the concrete so hard the rebound propelled me into the air. I told Tho, "In his previous life, Godzilla was a rodeo bull." I dragged my feet like hooves pawing the ground. "Kick like a bull."

"Bull!" He jumped and kicked his legs up behind him, the long colorful tail jouncing briskly, his squeals of joy ringing throughout the temple grounds. His excitement gave me a smile that made the muscles in my cheeks ache, elevating my cozy buzz to an even more exalted station.

We bull kicked our way around the pavilion, circling the Compassionate Mother. The fan dance girls lined up on our flanks, their bright silk dresses fluttering playfully, little legs kicking and stomping.

"It's the Year of the Horse, not the Bull," Ace said, breathy from the wild dancing.

Without pause I reared 'Zilla's head and let out a stallion's whinny. The girls giggled and went along with it, their tiny arms pawing the air, whinnying high-pitched, show ponies on sugar. Tho did a bang-up job swishing the tail, and even found two trash barrels to crash into, yelling his squeaky war cry with wild abandon. At that point our Godzilla dance was so enthralling that the trash scattered everywhere was just part of the show, confetti. Loud laughter and shocked gasps followed the booming clang of the toppled garbage cans.

I spun abruptly, spotting Miss Nguyen bending over a table to DJ the boom box. As she started a new song for us, I ran up behind her, 'Zilla's huge head shadowing her and the table, and let out a triumphant roar while mounting her. I grabbed her shoulders and dry humped her wide buttocks, which pulled the robe tightly around her leaning form.

It's possible I took it too far, letting her get a good feel of Godzilla's package, my Johnson pressing firmly between her warm cleft. *That's just wrong*, he twisted around. She shouted in surprise, but oddly made no attempt to fend me off. I roared and humped a few more times for good measure, enjoying the crowd's ludicrous response. From the corner of 'Zilla's mouth I spotted Blondie and Shocker standing next to each other, watching the show. The girl-beast had a hand to her mouth in utter disbelief. My girl just shook her head, grinning, filming the violation with her BlackBerry.

I dismounted and smacked her cheeks, *Thanks that was fun*, then turned and saw the fan girls were staring at their instructor with stunned O-shaped mouths. Miss Nguyen, still laying over the table, had a blush that looked like a bad sunburn. She breathed quickly, frozen with indecision. Pleasurable outrage. I kicked, bobbed my head, jumped, turned and wagged my whiskers. Ace had been a victim of the Giggle Monster throughout Miss Nguyen's ordeal. His laughter had regressed to snorts, wheezes and coughing, feet stumbling.

Someone in the congregation screamed suddenly. A bad scream. The cheers and raucous quieted instantly. Heads turned to look for the source. Miss Nguyen pushed herself off the table and turned the music off. Godzilla spun his head as well, no longer dancing. In the chilling silence our breathing inside the dragon became loud. Pandemonium ensued as gunfire cracked from the street, bullets scoring the tiles of the pavilion's roof, red chips spraying over the party, raining down on the concrete.

I cursed, ducked out of the dragon and caught cement in the face as the Compassionate Mother's arm was blown to shards by a stray round, shattering as it hit the ground. The children's screams were the loudest. People scrambled away from the pavilion, running for the safety of their temple.

Kids! Get the kids out of here, my subconscious spurred.

I turned and pointed at Tho, who stood next to the dragon with wide eyes. "Go! Inside the temple, now!" He nodded and ran.

Blondie and Shocker jogged up to me. My girl panted, "East End Boys."

"Who? Ace said, stopping next to his girl. He put a protective arm around her while squinting in the direction of the gang fight.

"They live across the street in those apartments." I pointed to the right. "Part of the Tiger Society."

"They are allies of the Two-Eleven and OBG," Blondie added.

"Fuckers," Shocker growled. "There are *kids* here."

"Where's Big guns?" I said. I scanned the empty pavilion area, the parking lot. *He'll be in the middle of the business*, I knew. "Come on!"

My crew followed me to the fence where Loc had stood in darkness earlier. I briefly wondered where he would be in all this. We jumped the low fence and crept through the church yard. We found the driveway and jogged to the road, crouching behind a large bush. The apartment complex across the street was two-storied, nothing fancy, small yellow-orange lights illuminating the doorways and stairs. The parking area on the side of the building was dark in places but I could clearly see numerous bodies jerking around in fighting postures. The sounds of men being punched and choked was an enticing scent in the cool, bustling breeze. An invitation.

Shocker opened the cargo pockets on her shorts, removed her brass knuckles and slipped them on her hands, making tight fists. Blondie was looking down at her boots, expensive new leather she didn't want to break in like this. She sighed and furrowed her perfectly plucked eyebrows. *Her Badass face really does it for me.*

"Where have you been?" Ace said to Bobby.

Big Swoll had just caught up to us, huge chest expanding and contacting with slow breaths. He looked at his geek friend with annoyance. "Making sure my wife and kids were safe, you Wheat Thin."

"Oh." Ace nodded.

"Babe, you're bleeding," Blondie said, suddenly turning to dab my face with tender fingers. She wiped the blood off my cheek. From the statue.

I shrugged, grabbed her hand. The sight of blood stirred the part of me that held the leash to my darker emotions. In the pitch black, my inner wolf was abruptly awake and too strong to restrain. My mouth closed and I became aware of her thumb in my mouth, tongue massaging the scarlet syrup off her pad.

I looked at my girl from under dark brows, with predator's eyes. She immediately responded with scared-thrilled arousal, ready to feel the rush of the hunt. *We are wolves*, my eyes burned. We can take down 1,000 lb. buffaloes.

"Hey," I said. My crew looked at me. "I don't know about you guys, but I feel like punching somebody." It took everything I had to present a calm face. The urge to bare canines and snarl was nearly overpowering.

"MFers ruined our party," Blondie said with passion. Tendons stood out from her biceps and neck. Fists clenched. Bright white teeth slightly showing behind pink, pissed lips. She made angry sexy.

Everyone seemed to be in agreement. I sniffed, took a deep breath, and motioned for us to go seek and destroy.

"Here we go again," Shocker said in a voice not her own. We took off running toward the apartments.

IX. A Long Ride

"Vagazzling," I proclaimed, motioning my hands like I was revealing a masterpiece to a gallery audience.

"Quit. You did your vagazzle presentation this morning. We don't have time to go through this again." Blondie looked down at me on my knees, the sink making her naked butt press out to the sides in a salivating squish of perfect skin. She examined her blonde pubbies critically. "I don't know. I think I like the exclamation point better." She tried to push me away with her bare feet, wanting to dress.

I grabbed her ankles in my hands, nibbled on a hot orange big toe. Said, "You don't like the flowers?" I looked at the design I had shaved on her this morning: two sunflowers, each about three inches long, complete with stems and leaves that intertwined. My trusty straight razor and I had carved them out like an Edward Scissorhands bush sculpture. To me it was priceless art one would labor over with great meticulous pain and present to a queen. I became contrary. "They're *much* more vagazzling than the simple exclamation mark."

She clucked her tongue. "It took too long." She kicked me away, hopped down and grabbed her panties off the floor.

"Wait. Wait wait wait." I stood and put my arms around her. *Again!* my Johnson flexed, ready for another go. *Convince her!*

"No! Raz, we have company." She put one foot in her panties.

I grabbed the Caribbean blue silk undergarment between my toes and pushed them back to the floor. "They can wait. It's me who can't..." I squeezed the back of her neck, brushing my lips down the front of it. Ran my tongue between her oh-yeahs, grabbing them lightly, squeezing, continuing with a trail of kisses down, down...

She grabbed my hair tightly with both hands, gripping it painfully. Her eyes closed. Moan escaping her open mouth.

Yes, my Johnson exulted. *Got her!*

I stood and pulled her legs around me, lifting her back onto the sink. Then changed my mind. *From the back this time.* Yeaaah.

Her eyes opened as I lifted her to turn her around. She looked down at my erection and snapped out of the spell. Pushed me away. "NO. We don't have another condom."

"So?" I murmured, leaning in to kiss the side of her neck.

Push. "No, man. You're not leaving a mess. You know the rule."

I groaned in defeat. Growled. I became aware of my dick retracting, though promising to fight again another day. I said, " 'When not at home, wear a rubber or get no pubbie fur.' " I blew out a breath. Let her go. "Fucking rules."

"*Hmmpt.*"

Fine. "Let's go suffer the social intercourse then, shall we?"

"Shut up." Her tone made me look like a whiny bitch. She slugged my shoulder. "When everyone leaves we'll go home and do another cardio session." She pulled her dress over her head. It glimmered blue in the shadow of her thick golden hair, silver in the harsh light of the bathroom.

I helped her with the shoulder straps, smiling at her phrase for our marathon sex sessions, looking forward to it. I turned to look for my underwear and remembered we had company and I would have to talk to them. "You have any mouthwash?"

"Of course, Señor Coochie Breath." She pointed at her handbag while slipping on black peep toes. Ran her tongue over her upper teeth. "I need that, too."

Yes you do, twitched the front of my boxer-briefs.

I put on my jeans and boots, buckled my belt and slipped into a white tee. Turned to inspect my hair in the mirror. Blondie touched up her face and hair with freakish speed and we walked out of the bathroom to continue hosting our friends, who were having lunch on the garage roof.

We walked up the ramp to the sixth level, concrete pillars like enormous sticks of chalk in the fluorescent lighting. The vault door was open, blue sky and puffy clouds the first thing visible as our just-had-an-orgasm steps floated us onto the freshly swept roof. The sun was bright, though not hot. Perfect afternoon. My crew plus Perry, the Elder Dragon and Big Guns sat at the picnic tables between the two sheds, the canopy rolled back to allow the autumn sunlight to lend its healthy rays to the cookout. It was the first time we've used the area for company, and I now knew why Blondie insisted on more than one table. *She was planning on something like this all along*, I thought with a suspicious glance at her.

Buff paint and polished wheels shot glares into our eyes from my Hayabusa, Blondie's truck and Ace's and Big Guns' imports. Classic rock jammed at a low volume from the open doors of Perry's '49 GMC. Our coach's brother stood in front of my gas grill, stainless steel lid open, steaks, hamburgers and hot dogs sizzling. Thick meaty scents swirled around the tables. Shocker, sitting next to her man on a bench, held their baby daughter in her lap with one hand while helping her cut a hot dog with a fork. The not-quite two year old had chubby cheeks, brunette pigtails, and a cute pug nose just like her mother's.

"Barbie-Q dog!" the little girl said, and stabbed a chunk of Oscar Meyer off a paper plate, dipped it in "Barbie-Q" sauce, then painted the shoulder of her purple dress and both cheeks before getting it in her mouth. The fork looked huge in her itty-bitty pink fingers.

Shocker *yayed* her daughter's success, then looked at me and Blondie like she was about to say something. She gasped in surprise instead, looking down at the sauce-loaded hot dog her kid had dropped onto the front of her tight white running shirt. Blondie thought it was the cutest thing and *ahh'd*. Bobby and Big Guns wisely refrained from voicing their humor while the two older men boomed laughter. The Shocker glowered in their direction. Ace took his daughter while the girl-beast stood with arms out to her sides and stomped off to the bathroom spitting curses to herself.

I looked at my girl, jerked my head at Shocker's tense back, *You want that in your life?*

She cut her eyes away from me, *Whatever!*

Blondie took a spot next to her stocky Viet pal while I slipped onto the bench next to *Anh Long*. They were paying attention to the grill master. Perry's white Hot Rod Magazine shirt and khaki shorts fluttered in the gentle gusts of sea breeze as he told a story. I grabbed a paper plate from a stack next to the burgers and fixings, listening to his rumbling tone as I assembled my grub.

"...And I got pulled over! I didn't realize how fast I was going," he said, sunglassed face alternating between his task of turning meat and looking at us. "So I stopped and the cop came to my window. 'What's the rush?' the asshole said. I hung my arm and head out the window to get a good look at the kid." He looked at *Anh Long*. "He was an overzealous muscle head with a high-and-tight and aviator shades."

Anh Long grunted. "Police academy cookie-cutter."

That made us laugh. Perry stuck out his under bite in a grin, continued. "I told him, 'Look, I'm a nurse. I was called to the ER for an emergency. You're gonna have to hurry this up.'" He twirled the tongs in his immense hand. "Someone could lose their life." He acted out the cop's body language, hand on gun, face skeptical. "But the guy wouldn't listen. Asshole acted like I was lying."

"Were you?" I said before inhaling a quarter of my cheeseburger in one bite.

"No," he rumbled, scowling. "The cop wanted to know what I did at the hospital. By that time I was mad. So I told him, 'I stretch assholes.'"

Ace snickered. Blondie looked at the baby, deciding whether to scold him for cursing in front of the child. Her dislike of cops took precedence and she stopped fidgeting and listened to our coach's bro' finish his story. I burped slightly and said, "So then he wanted to know what the hell you meant by that."

Perry nodded. "I told him, 'I use a finger at time, then a hand at a time. I stretch and stretch until the assholes are open to a full six feet.' " He held his hands apart wide.

The Elder Dragon and Big Guns both looked confused, as if this was some kind of Caucasian humor they didn't understand. I had stopped chewing, unable to see where this was going. Ace was rapt, not seeming to notice his girl sit down next to him and take the baby back.

Perry tongued several hot dogs onto a large plate next to the grill. "This guy knew I was pulling his leg. He was mad. We were *both* mad. He asked me, 'What the hell do you do with a six-foot asshole?' " Perry pulled down his sunglasses and looked at us over the rims. "I told him, 'We assign them a badge and a patrol car.' "

The two Asian men swayed with laughter, heads nodding vigorously. The punch line caught the rest of us so off-guard we were hit with full-fledged giggle-cramps-wheeze attacks. Abs burned. Eyes watered. Food was dropped. I forgot I had burger in my mouth and choked on it. That was possibly the best verbal punch in a cop's face I've ever heard.

Anh Long was the first to get his wits back. He gestured at Perry in a manner that seemed to convey, *Thank you for the entertainment. Now please listen to my story.* He beckoned to the rest of us, his drawn down mouth and darkening eyes making us feel things were about to get serious.

The old man leaned forward on his elbows, glanced at his *Em Hung*. Big Guns looked back uneasily. *Anh Long* said to us, "I have many things I need to tell you, some of it recently learned. Though first I must thank you on behalf of the temple." He clasped his hands together and gave us a slight bow. "Those troubled young men could have caused more harm to our people had you not assisted our security." He motioned a hand at Big Guns.

I shrugged, *No problem.* "The East End Boys were overdue for a tune-up. It was only a matter of time before we paid them a visit, anyhow."

He waved off my nonchalance. "You risked your lives."

"They deserved every busted eye and fractured bone," Shocker said, venomous. The baby picked up on her sudden shift in mood and began crying. Ace took her, shushing gently, rubbing her back.

I smiled at the memory. We were Baddists among Buddhists, the unmerciful lords of combat tearing into the thug scrubs like prime dire wolves attacking a pack of mangy coyotes. Though they submitted in terror, I knew there was unfinished business. *Which we'll handle*, I mused with an arrogant lift of my head.

"Humph," *Anh Long* put a finger to his lips, looking between me and the girl-beast. "Whenever possible, I try to determine what caused the behavior of those that offend me. With understanding comes forgiveness, and life moves on without being held back by vendettas. The East End Boys are dinghies being towed by a ship with an unstable captain. Diep has limited control of himself, and his direction of the Tiger Society's lower rungs reflects that."

"Where is he, anyway?" Bobby said from behind a tall glass of iced tea. His bright yellow tank top matched his stretch pants, body builder wear that glowed over his dark skin.

"We'll get to that," Big Guns told him.

The Elder Dragon nodded to Big Swoll with a smile, *please be patient*. He said to me, "Everyone was, ah, intrigued by your style of dragon dancing." He pulled at the neck of his shirt, an oriental-style button-up, white with no collar.

"Godzilla dancing," I clarified.

"Godzilla? Well that explains the trash barrels," *Anh Long* muttered.

"I told Miss Nguyen that was part of the show." Blondie looked apologetic. She turned evil eyes on me. "Before I picked up the mess his showmanship left."

"Hey, the tail did that. Tho helped clean up." I showed everyone my #1 Mr. Good Guy face. "My goal was to get everyone's blood pumping." I put a hand on my chest, all innocence. "I feel like I did my job."

"Pfff." Shocker wagged her ponytail. "You pumped more than someone's blood."

I showed her all my teeth. "Yes, I did."

"Regardless of your pumping tactics," *Anh Long* said smiling at Shocker. He looked at me. "We believe it was well-intentioned, and quite entertaining. Sometimes a break in tradition is what everyone needs." He hummed a nod for emphasis.

I mugged the girls, *Ha! What do you know?*

Everyone ate slowly, sipping tea while the head of the Dragon Family stood to stretch his back. He clasped his hands behind him, addressing us all. "Diep is a bad enemy to have. Make no mistake. He will be around again to cause more trouble."

"He's in Houston right now," Ace said. I noticed his hand rubbing the side of his leg, caressing a large Velcro pocket containing a modified Galaxy *Note.* He glanced at Bobby, who frowned, *Why didn't you tell me?*

Anh Long looked thoughtful. "Our source says he will be in New Orleans imminently, and will send a team of enforcers to Biloxi to search for you." He rubbed a scar on one of his long brown fingers. "Diep does not wish to return because the police seek him for questioning."

"Is your source reliable?" Shocker asked. "Are they close to Diep?"

Anh Long gave an eyes-closed-smiling nod. "Reliable information is what wins the war. The Tiger Society may win battles with guns and muscles, but information, used strategically, will ultimately triumph."

The "source" was apparently news to Big Guns. He looked at his *Anh Hai* beseechingly. "Anyone I know?" The old man nodded without elaborating. Big Guns' jaw muscles bulged.

I pointed at the girl-beast. "Anyone she punched?" She twisted her lips, narrowed her eyes, *Take this more seriously, idiot.* I pointed my chin at her, swiped the back of my fingers under my jaw, flicking them in her direction.

"One of Diep's personal security, yes," *Anh Long* said to me. "I believe you have met. He has been ordered to fight for Diep. That is why *Em Hung* has been forbidden from shooting-to-kill. We have other men in their organization, men with families." He held his ancient fists up. "We can hurt them with these." He made a finger pistol. "But we must risk bullets only when absolutely necessary."

Big Guns showed his displeasure at being forbidden from killing the enemy. Shocker stroked her baby's soft hair, smiling down at her. In a pleasant, almost musical voice, she said, "Diep is welcome to try again." Somehow, her melodious tone made the statement more profound. The baby giggled up at her silly mommy.

"He will," *Anh Long* told her. "Diep is stubborn, and very vengeful. His treachery is notorious. And he does not hesitate to pursue those he feels crossed the Tiger Society. Everyone who has confronted him is either dead or under his thumb, paying for it with blood or sweat. He will bide his time, devise a plan, and attack when you least expect it. The man is unstable, but very cunning."

"Has the Two-Eleven or OBG tried to move in on D'Iberville again?" Blondie wanted to know, tapping a napkin to her lips. She stood to gather plates and refill drinks.

Anh Long shook his head. "They will try again one day, maybe. The extortion rackets weren't viewed as very important to the Tiger Society. They were just something for the *thang ca chon* to do."' He shrugged. "Without a competent captain, the Two-Eleven and Oriental Baby Gangsters are incapable of orchestrating a successful racket. Their intimidation methods are wasteful, very inefficient. The upper echelons of the Tiger Society make use of them but allow them their own exploits without much supervision."

"What's their primary income?" I asked. "If they aren't making anything from the loan-and-take game, where is all their cash coming from? Those boys have more than pocket-change." I finished off my burger and sucked down some tea, watching the old man carefully.

The Elder Dragon looked disturbed. He glanced at the baby in a way that made my spine abruptly straighten. He said, "About half of their income is from distribution of cocaine and ecstasy. The other half is from trafficking."

Blondie frowned. "I didn't know they were drivers."

"No, Babe." I glanced at him, at the baby. "I think he means human trafficking."

He confirmed my assumption by not correcting me. Shocker and Bobby took the news badly. She unconsciously put a protective arm around the little girl. Big Swoll blew out an angry breath and stood. Walked over to the roof's edge and stared down at the highway and beach. My girl and I just looked at the old man. He said, "I knew Diep's father in Vietnam. Never known another man so immoral. He was stealing and selling children to sex houses in Thailand." He looked like he wanted to spit. "It is known that Diep was exposed to this."

"Exposed?" I said. "Was he abused?"

He nodded as if sick. "When Diep was six, his father sold him to Thai pirates."

Blondie gripped my arm and gasped. Damn. Suddenly I felt bad for the sorry MFer. And something told me this tale was going to get much worse. "Pirates," I muttered. "That explains his temper." I rubbed my leg, recalling Diep's psycho soccer kick.

"I think the loss of his *schlong* is the reason for that," Ace said. "They made him a eunuch sex slave for the men on the boats."

Anh Long looked at the geek in surprise. "You are well-informed."

"I found some transcripts from Immigration Control, from the eighties," he replied. His girl looked at him, *Why didn't you tell me?* He shrugged, *Sorry.*

I'll have to talk to him about communicating as a crew, I mentally sighed.

The Elder Dragon said, "Some Vietnamese refugees told very sad stories to elicit sympathy from U.S. officials, hoping to get citizenship. However, most of the stories were true. Diep had it worse than most of us that left Asia, but has it better than any of us in America. He was taken in by a wealthy family and went to college."

"What did he major in?" I inquired. "Punk Motherfuckerism?"

The old man frowned at me. "Business."

Everyone liked my quip except the girl-beast. She sighed exasperation, then said to *Anh Long*, "What about you? Last night you told me you escaped the Vietnamese Communists in your boat. Did your family leave with you?"

He nodded, cleared his throat. Intertwined his fingers on top of the table and stared at the condensation beading on the glass in front of him. "My wife and I knew if we didn't leave we would die in Vietnam. We also knew we would be killed if they caught us leaving. The thought of true freedom trumped thoughts of consequences, and we liquidated all our possessions for a bar of gold, which I hid on my boat. We packed only necessities, hoping the little food and water we brought would last for the two-day trip to Thailand. Six other people from our village came with us. Two were children. Orphans. One was an old woman; she nearly died from the stress of hiking to the boat. Two were men my age, one with a young wife. We left one night and got away. The next day, far away from any land, we were attacked by Thai pirates. Everyone knew this may happen. It was common, unfortunately. They beat me and the other men badly. They tore up our engine and took our food and water. Then they took two of our women."

He cleared his throat again. "I was unconscious when they took my wife off the boat. When I came to, I didn't know what had happened. The old woman was bathing my head wounds. The others were sobbing. I could hear screams on the wind." His voice broke. "My wife's screams. She was fighting them as they raped her. Then they shot her and her terror was silenced."

We were stunned by his story. He took a drink, we took a breath. Then he continued, "The current pushed her body back in our direction. I used the anchor and rope to pull her in, fighting off the others to do so. I was scaring the children. Hysterical with grief."

I glanced at the baby clinging to Shocker's neck, eyes wide and frightened as she watched the old man, sensitive to the grown-ups' mood. *You're scaring the children now,* I thought. Then, *Damn, at least the pirates didn't steal those orphans.*

Shocker looked extremely sorry for having asked about his escape story. She was unlikely to inquire about the fate of the second woman they took. *Anh Long* looked at her with new emotion, eyes watery. The uncharacteristic display made everyone highly uneasy. Voice choked, he whispered, "When I pulled my wife into the boat her legs were missing."

He lay his head on his hands, neck tense, holding back a sob. The girls teared up, walking over to console him. He waved them off, then gestured to the stoic Big Guns to say something while he recovered.

I looked at my girl, at her legs that had just been wrapped around me.

What would you do if a school of sharks ate them? my subconscious dared to ask.

I shuddered in answer.

The intense tale had everyone on edge. Shocker wiped her eyes and made happy mommy sounds to ward off the crying fit the baby's face foretold. Big Guns looked at me like, *Shit man. That's life.* He was Ged-up in baggy jeans and a dark red Hilfiger long-sleeve, gold rope chain and rings blinging as bright as his silver grill. He was all business, refocusing our party on what was relevant. In his slightly gruff accent he said, "Diep had a bad childhood, but he gets no pass for the way he is now. He's had many chances to make things right, but he's incapable. *No ac lam,*" he's evil. He took out a pack of Newports, lit one and inhaled with a contemplative expression.

Ace was impatient for more information. The hard drive of his mind whirred behind his eyes, one squinted with abnormal intelligence. He was eager to start researching our next job. "Tell us more about the trafficking," he implored the gangster.

Big Guns looked around to see if everyone was done processing the last exchange. We turned to him. He said, "In the last four years the number of missing children on the Coast has risen. They are mostly illegals, unknown to the authorities, so they aren't missed. The parents are illegals so they rarely file missing persons reports."

The girls showed him faces that strongly disagreed with the children not being missed. He waved his cigarette placating. "They aren't missed by the *government*, who does nothing because they aren't citizens."

"Uncle Sam only makes an effort for U.S. citizens because they fear bad press," I said, a taste of anarchy curling my tongue.

He nodded seriously. "Most of the kids I'm speaking of are Viet and Mexican, some of them just babies. What's interesting is another number that's risen at the same time." Grunt. "Diep's bank account."

Ace palmed his Galaxy *Note,* reading from the tablet's screen. "Three accounts in the Caymans. Two in Houston, which is where the Tiger Society is headquartered. He has small business accounts in Oakland and Baltimore as well. He's chairman of the Society's fourteen corporate buildings in the U.S., and personally owns one building in Toronto. Numerous houses and condos. All under aliases, of course, fronted by a dummy corporation that's completely legit on paper. He has brilliant accountants, I'll give him that." He shook his head, looking like a gamer that had his skills mildly taxed to complete a level.

"But not too brilliant for my man." Shocker leaned over and smooched him. The baby yanked on her hair, cutting it short.

Anh Long, Perry and Big Guns looked at the geek with superstitious expressions. The rest of us were impressed, but we were used to his extraordinary skill. I said, "Where are the kids going?"

Big Guns blew out a long stream of smoke, still looking at Ace and his tablet. "The Tiger Society has factions in most major cities. The kids are shipped all over. Some are forced to join gangs, though most are put to work."

"Slaves," Bobby growled. The single word transformed him. Veins swelled in his arms, neck, the touchy subject putting creases around his dark eyes and mouth. He squeezed his fists tight, knuckles popping ominously.

Big Guns nodded with his own menace. "If they are lucky they end up sweeping floors and doing laundry. If they are unlucky... I don't have to tell you how they end up." He grunted darkly.

Shocker couldn't take any more bad news. She had a tempestuous vigor about her, ugly mad. She stood and handed the baby to Ace, walked around the grill with clenched jaw. Perry eyed her with concern as he raked the grill clean with a wire brush. She turned to face the Asian men, sun producing a halo around her dark hair. *Or is that steam rising from her ears?* She said, "Well, I can tell you how Diep will end up..." Her lips quivered, eyes shutting tight.

Perry started to reach over and put a comforting hand on her shoulder but thought better of it. The woman's teeth were bared, and I got the feeling all her willpower was directed at containing her darker persona from coming out. *Fight junkie, she called it.* She barked a frustrated growl, spun on a toe and walked over to stand next to Bobby. The giant had turned back to the highway, listening to the disturbing news while watching the congested traffic inch along.

Ace knew better than to console his girl when she had her hackles up. He bounced the baby on his leg, looked over at Blondie and made a decent attempt to lift the negative atmosphere. "Did you see her new tattoo?" He inclined his head at Shocker.

Blondie nodded, smiling a little. Looked over at her. "Said she got it in Juarez."

The girl-beat's left shoulder shined with ointment, moisturizer for the freshly inked skin. PERNICIOUS was written in pretty script in an arch above several flowers and vines that weaved through golden brass knuckles. A large, thick scar was below it, an obvious bullet wound. Blondie smirked with envy. Said, "Yeah. Bad mofo. Fits her perfectly."

"Pernicious?" Big Guns looked quizzical. He looked at me and smiled. "I saw she had a new tat, but every time I thought to ask her about it she looked angry about something." He grunted humorously. "What does it mean? You know gangsters don't read much." Broad gleam of silver.

"Means very destructive, injurious," I answered. The fancy letters and flowers cloaked the word's dynamic meaning. Just like her pretty exterior cloaked her violent interior. Blondie was right. That tattoo fit her even better than the Champion spark plug. She calls her left fist "Seek," her right fist "Destroy," and they are certainly very destructive, injurious.

"Crap," Ace mumbled. He sniffed his daughter and chuckled. Literally. He glanced at us. Reached under the table and grabbed a large pink and white diaper bag, stood and slung it over a shoulder. Hefted the baby. "I'll be back. Caroline needs to be freshened up."

Caroline. That's her damn name, I thought. Blondie smiled at the geek, at the baby. She glanced at me with meaning. I had a sudden urge to run and jump off the roof. *I'm not changing any diapers, woman,* my shaking head told her.

"*Hmmpt.*" We'll see.

Children's laughter made us turn toward the roof entrance. Tho and Carl shuffled through the vault door with push brooms held up like swords, clacking them together with shouts of "Yaw!" Tho looked like a street urchin once more, thin dingy pants and torn shirt hardly wearable, sandals looking like dog chew toys. His snaggled grin and happy squeals were mirrored by his new friend.

Carl was a much more confident kid than the one we found by the highway with the shame sign around his neck. He was a couple of years older than Tho, but not much bigger. His Spider Man shirt was as faded as his jeans, dusty from sweeping parking slots. Their Dragon Ball Z play fight *clacked* its way over in front of the laboratory shed. Everyone grinned at them. The swinging broom handles so near to 'Zuki were beginning to make me nervous. I started to say something but the old man beat me to it.

"*Tho, troi nhieu qua. Quet don di!*" You play too much, Tho. Sweep up, *Anh Long* scolded.

Carl didn't understand the language, though recognized a scolding when he heard one. His smile vanished with Tho's. They stood with brooms in front of them, abashed. *Or pretending to be,* I mused to myself.

Blondie had walked over to them. Ruffled Carl's hair. "You guys had enough to eat?"

"Yes, ma'am," Carl replied, looking up at her in worship.

"Yeah," Tho said. He glanced at the Elder Dragon and corrected himself. "Yes, ma'am."

"Good. When you finish for the day I'll get you some ice cream."

"Yay!" the boys exclaimed. Blondie beamed at their response.

Shocker brought the working men glasses of tea. "I may have to hire you boys to do some work at my place." She seemed eager and grateful for the distraction.

Tho and Carl thanked her, then turned their glasses up with both hands, one eye on each other, racing to see who could finish the quickest. They drained the cold tea, gasped for air. Tho set his glass on a table, palmed his broom off his shoulder and thumped it on the concrete. "I won!"

"Nuh-uh," Carl argued. "*I* won."

"Back to work," Big Guns said. They looked at him. He pointed an imperative finger. "Stay where Cong and Tuan can see you," he commanded, referring to his security leaders positioned north and south of the garage. They were competent men, in charge of eight others that covered a wide perimeter around the block. The boys acknowledged and ran off, their piping voices echoing as they went down the ramp, renewing their Dragon Ball identities.

Shocker had her equilibrium back, holding Caroline on her hip. The large wet spot on the front of her shirt - the one she had just changed into - made me frown at the baby. Her mother absently fended off hair-grasping hands and walked over to stand on the other side of the table from *Anh Long*. Said to him, "Loc's accomplishments in the military must make you proud."

The Elder Dragon gave a faint smile. "My son has many talents. Most are useful while unknown." He warmed to the subject, eyes thankful for the shift in mood. "He was proficient with a rifle even as a little boy. He loved BB guns. And he was always good at traveling without detection, through woods, neighborhoods, and such."

Shocker pursed her lips. "No wonder."

They chatted while I became lost in thought. Last night Loc had climbed to the roof of the apartments to give us cover. He must've had a night vision scope. He shot guns from the enemies' hands, then managed to hold off several Biloxi PD by taking out their tires. The cops were three blocks away when their cruisers took fire. They jumped out and took cover, which gave us plenty of time to finish scuffing up the East End Boys and get away. *How did Loc get away?* The entire police force had shown up. "The guy should star in his own Tom Clancy novel," I proclaimed.

"Patterson," Bobby rumbled in disagreement.

"James Patterson?" I queried. "Why?"

Everyone looked at Big Swoll. He said, "Clancy only does white boys. Patterson does everybody."

I shrugged.

Ace put his tablet on the table and pushed the touch screen to play some music. Rick James, of all people. Bobby's bright smile and nodding head was contagious, and soon nearly all of us were making funky sounds or jigging our shoulders to the party jam. Blondie and Perry picked up the food and stored it in the lab's 'fridge while I wiped down everything with Lysol.

The girls bokked, the men bluhhed. Tho and Carl played hyperactively. The socializing was getting out of hand. Since there was no drinking or drugging I just observed, wishing they would cease this madness. Stop *sharing* so much.

"*Mmmarrgh*," I groaned. *Fucking feelings...* What's up with that? I walked over and pushed pause on the geek's tablet, drawing everyone's attention. I held my hands up, fingertips touching, trying not to scowl. "Lovely party, people. Thanks for coming." My girl gave a cynical snort. The girl-beast narrowed her eyes. My fingers took it upon themselves to show them double fuck-yous. The boys snickered. I said, "I believe we should keep the momentum rolling. You know you're ready for the next phase of operation Seek and Destroy." Shocker gave me a look mixed with surprise and unexpected appreciation. I nodded to her with complete belief in our team. *That's right. It's like that.*

Anh Long looked at me piercingly. "Tell us what you have in mind."

* * *

Perry's GMC looked and sounded like an iron god on supernatural 'roids. When Shocker secured Caroline's car seat in it the monster

Henry Roi

'49 seemed to dwindle in stature, losing the "hot" in its rodding personality. I instantly felt sorry for it. "I'll take good care of the little princess, don't worry," Perry assured the parents, grinning down at his tiny passenger.

The 454 ignited, concrete vibrating under our shoes. The cam loped tones that suggested the truck was aware of its precious cargo and didn't approve. Our Coach's bro' waved jovially and idled off. Shocker watched the tailgate go down the ramp with worry before getting into the Scion with her man and Big Swoll.

The Viet crime bosses jumped into the Prelude, and the tricked out imports tailed Blondie and me in the Ford, racing down the levels of the garage, onto Highway 90. Tho and Carl waved from the street entrance, Cong and Tuan standing sentry behind them, faces deadpan and watchful. I assumed Big Guns' other security guys were scrambling to vanguard their organization leaders to our destination.

Since Blondie screwed up by posting pics on the 'Net, I no longer had to freeze on 'Zuki for the winter, which made the long ride down the chilly beach to Biloxi pleasant. To stave off boredom I gave my lovely blonde lynx a patient, affectionate massage. My attempt at a happy ending was ruined, though.

She was right on the verge of voicing the crossing of her Finish line when we were cut off by some redneck in a dump truck. The frustrating break in her concentration and panicked stomp on the brakes caused her to growl and curse and flip him off. She shoved me away, rolled down her window and yelled curses over the wind and dump truck's noisy drive train, threatening to track down and castrate the fucker. Then she cut *him* off, and I hung my naked white ass out the window to show support for my girl's road rage. Horns honked. I wiggled my cheeks, singing along to Three Days Grace, Cerwin Vegas behind the seats thundering, anus tingling pleasantly from the 90 mph wind buffeting my crack. The window frame dug into my hip from the 429's acceleration.

Blondie's boutique was a small business in a strip mall off Pass Road. She owned the building, leasing six of the eight facilities to local proprietors that offered everything from manicures to deli sandwiches. Customers trickled in and out of the long white brick and stucco businesses. I spotted two of Big Guns' guys as we turned into the parking area, known by their red and gold Infinity G37s. I assumed they were coordinating with their crew, reporting the security of the area before Big Guns and the Elder Dragon even turned off the highway.

The double glass doors reflected our badass selves and the sun-refracting cars behind us. I opened one, held it for my squad and our Viet allies that waited until everyone went in before jogging to the entrance from the Prelude. A grim, thirty-something gangster in a tie-less suit named Gat posted up on the walk just outside the door, ignoring my circumspection, watching the people get in and out of their vehicles immediately in front of us, and over in front of the second building in the plaza, a machine shop and restaurant combination. I observed everything for a few more seconds, feeling a touch of paranoia I couldn't rationalize.

You're sober, genius, my subconscious murmured, partially in complaint.

I chalked it up to that, walked inside, door hissing shut behind me.

My eyes adjusted from the sun to the drop ceiling cool glow of LEDs. Being her man, I could tell this was Blondie's store just from the items on display. Glass shelves and stands were positioned on the walls and floor so that aisles slanted across the utterly feminine room like glossy, colorful, perfumed artwork. Baskets of soaps, candles and bath beads were on the left in front, fresh flower arrangements perched in the back corner, flanking a counter full of female Viagra (AKA "jewelry") and clothing racks of quality jackets, purses, and mouth-watering bra and pantie sets.

In the center was a huge aquarium with floral colored lights. The wall of mirrors behind it doubled the volume of the flowers and fish, giving the feeling of paradise to adult customers, while imbibing mirth in the children who liked to peck on the glass and tease the guppies as their mothers shopped for lingerie, nail polish, opal-adorned handbags and hats. I walked past a wide-hipped woman holding a small dog, glanced at the empty cashier counter on the right, heading through the short hallway to the coffee bar.

"You have a customer in front," Blondie told Crystal with a smile undertoned with reproof. She flipped hair off her forehead, pert nose turned up, glanced at Shocker, who sat on a stool between Ace and Bobby, elbows on the glossy granite bar. *Anh Long* and his protégé took seats at one of the two booths, watching the anxious teenager sweat under her boss' scrutiny.

Crystal hurriedly finished restocking paper cups next to an array of shiny coffee makers. "Sorry, ma'am. I'm by myself today. Tommy never showed." She scurried around the bar, smiled pleasantly at our friends, a stunning platinum blonde seventeen-year-old in a green sundress with a heart-shaped name badge. "I'll be right back if you guys need anything!" she said cheerily before hurrying through the hallway.

"Tommy," Blondie growled darkly, staring at a grease board mounted above the coffee machines. Employee schedules. "Little son of a bitch."

"Gotta fire him?" Shocker inquired.

Blondie walked behind the bar, took out some espresso cups. Sighed. "No. His mom is a friend of mine."

"Ooh! Ooh! Can I talk to him?" I raised my hand for permission.

Blondie rolled her eyes. "Geez." Humming sigh. "I guess so."

"Oh, goodie-goodie-goodie. Thanks, Babe." I rubbed my palms together. I've been waiting a long time to give Tommy an attitude adjustment.

Shocker turned creased brows on me. "You better not intimidate some little kid."

I scowled at her, *Mind your own business, turd.*

"Don't worry," Blondie laughed. "Tommy is nearly as big as Bobby." Big Swoll felt that comment called for a quick biceps flex. "And, it's not so much intimidation as dynamic motivation. Raz is good at making people aware of the consequences of slacking. He's very persuasive with his life lessons."

"Oh." Shocker quirked her lips, not sure if she was impressed, surprised, or still in the mood to mean mug me.

Blondie served tasty, hot espresso while I watched Crystal serve a couple of yuppies in the front. Whenever I accompany my girl to the boutique, I'll try to work with her employees on their salesmanship. Principles like Association, Reciprocation, Scarcity and Consistency were valuable to know for any retail business. Crystal was a quick learner, though wasn't very eager to implement sales tactics she felt were "icky." But that was okay; I didn't mind prodding her into doing it. *She needs to learn it's dog-eat-dog*, I smiled to myself. Then beckoned, "Pssst!"

She looked at me, *Huh?*

I rolled a finger, *Let's do the thing.*

She shook her head, *Uh-uh.*

Emphatic roll of finger, scowl. *Let's. Do. The. Thing.*

Exasperated sigh, *Oh, all right!*

A few minutes later a late-forties ego in a tight cadmium yellow skirt approached the counter with a bright yellow handbag. "How much is this?" she asked Crystal, looking down her nose at the peasant.

"Oh, like, um, I'm not sure," Crystal dumb-blonded her. "I'll have to ask my manager."

Arrogant sigh. "I don't have all day, girl." She tapped an expensive shoe. Fingered her three-hundred dollar hairdo.

Crystal turned to look at me. "Um, sir? How much for this handbag?"

Blondie, face behind my neck with a grin I wanted to match but couldn't let the mark see, whispered, "Thirty-nine dollars."

"Sixty-two dollars," I said loudly.

Crystal frowned, looked at the customer apologetically. Looked back at me. "I'm sorry. I couldn't hear you." She leaned slightly in my direction, straining to make her inept blonde brain hear me.

"Sixty-two dollars!" I shouted.

I grabbed Blondie's hand and we hooved it around the bar with suppressed giggles, waved for everyone to join us in watching the camera monitors underneath. On the screen showing the checkout desk, Crystal had turned back to the impatient rich bitch. She smiled and chirped stupidly, "Fifty-two dollars."

The customer's foot quit tapping. The hallway monitor showed her crane her neck to peer into the coffee bar. Then she quickly handed Crystal her credit card, signed for the purchase, and strutted her crooked ass out of the boutique with a new handbag she'll tell everyone some imbecile sold her for ten dollars less than cost.

Hmm-hmm-HMM! My inner-crook gloated. *You over paid, bitch.*

"What just happened?" Shocker's mouth was open. "Did you just scam that lady?"

"Nope." My canines lengthened. "She scammed us."

"How... *What???*"

"She may not have bought it. We simply presented her a deal she couldn't pass up."

"But she thinks she..."

"Ripped us off for ten bucks?" I expressed offense. "Damn broad stole from us. I hope she comes back and does it again."

"Razor believes everyone has the capacity to steal." Big Guns told Shocker, Ace and Bobby.

"Larceny is in everybody," I agreed, sipping my espresso.

Silver smile. "So every once in a while he creates a scenario that brings out the thieving monkey in all of us." He grunted. "I think he just likes to fuck with people."

"Thieving monkey," *Anh Long* muttered humorously, shaking his head.

I threw my empty cup in the trash. "Everyone has stolen something at some point in their life. It's in our nature. Even old Christian grandmas like to beat the system out of a few bucks. That lady," I pointed to the front doors, "clearly heard me say sixty-two dollars. Yet she hurried up and paid fifty-two and left before the mistake was discovered. *Greeed.*" I ruffled Crystal's hair as she brushed past me, pulling it loose from clips and whatnot. "I love it! Good job, Grasshopper."

Crystal froze in her walk, blinking in disbelief. She clenched her fists, stomped a sandal. "Mister Man! It took me for-*ever* to get that right." She patted her 'do. "Oh my GOD."

"You have my permission to hit him," Blondie said, taking a dainty sip of espresso, one eyebrow arched.

"Mine too," Shocker added.

The men looked at me like, *You're on your own with that one, pal.* Crystal *ughed* me once more, stomping off to the ladies' room. I pointed and hollered at her. "Hey! I just made you a thirteen dollar tip. You're lucky I don't make you split it!"

"Forget you, Mister Man!" her muffled voice spat from the hall.

"All right. Well. That was fun." I clapped my hands once, faced the room. "Now that my inner-crook has enjoyed a taste, he wants more. Shall we go add a few more ingredients to our criminal brew?" I motioned for everyone to follow me. They got up, the men smirking, women shaking their pretty heads, followed me into the hallway.

The door opposing the bathrooms accessed the business next door. Emotion Art. Another of my girl's excellent enterprises. It was closed today, all appointments canceled because we needed to get some things and do some things without witnesses. The new carpet smell was strong after huffing the perfume and coffee ambience of the boutique. Blondie took point. I closed the door after everyone filed through.

Emotion Art had the same floor space as the business we had just left, though it was configured differently. The front had a desk by the entrance, facing four small chambers with soundproof walls and thick steel doors, each with a stylishly scripted sign designating their purpose. From left to right: Chapel, Sensory Deprivation, Video, and Audio. Blondie gave a tour and elaborated on the business model.

"You guys know what a Rorschach test is?" she asked as they looked at the chambers curiously.

"Those old ink-blot flash cards. Doctors showed them to patients and asked what they saw," Ace answered.

"I like those," Bobby said. "Little miniature Jackson Pollock paint-ings."

"Mmm-hmm," Blondie agreed, flashing a grin at the giant. "They are paintings that elicit emotion. What I've done here," she waved at the rooms, "is reverse that concept. Emotion elicits paintings."

"How?" Shocker was fully intrigued.

Blondie opened the Audio room. The heavy door unlatched loudly, pulled open silently. She nodded into the chambers. "Electroen-cephalography."

"EEG? *Awesome.*" Ace's eyes were screens televising the *Geek Show.* "I had an EEG when I was twelve and studying neuroscience. I used it to scan the brain waves of dogs and cats while they were eating and sleeping, or playing in aggressive states -"

"Pusssht." Shocker pinched his lips together. Smiled, shaking her head gently.

"Yes, dear." He shrugged apologetically to Blondie. Received a quick kiss from his girl.

Blondie's eyes broadcasted her own brand of Nerd TV. Feeling like a boy lusting on his science teacher, I focused on her foxy gestures. She said, "An electrode cap is placed on the customer's head so that the EEG can scan the brain's cortex. Every thought, action, or feeling has its own unique wave signature." They nodded in understanding. I stuck my hand in my pocket to pinch the arousal out of my Johnson.

But she's so hot when she talks smart! he argued.

I pinched harder, *Later,* and he squirmed, attempting to dislodge my submission hold.

She went on, unaware of my plight. "These wave signatures are con-verted into digital code by an algorithm, which determines what color, shape, density or speed the airbrush 'bot paints."

"Wait," Bobby said, arms crossed, one large finger aimed at her. "There's a painting *robot* in there?" He pointed at the chamber.

Huge perfect smile. "I have four of them. Look." They eyed the inte-rior of the Audio room. The door and walls were covered with rows of tiny pyramids, sound dampers that isolated a customer's senses from the outside. In this room people listened to their favorite songs while the apparatus created art from the emotions. Upbeat songs excite the cortex and create paintings with fast sweeps and lively colors, showing the energy felt by the music. Melodramatic songs produce gloomy renderings, sweeping grays and blues. And so on. It was surprisingly accurate.

A white leather recliner sat in the center facing the door. White being a neutral color, had little influence on the mind. A small stand next to it with drawers contained headphones and differently sized EEG caps. The back wall was a sheet of thick, clear Plexiglas, showcasing the robot and easel beyond it. The 'bot was cylindrical, titanium, about the size of a large fire extinguisher. Highly polished. It had five arms: two on each side, one in the center, triple-jointed with tiny hydraulics, hoses, servo motors and airbrushes for "hands." A color was assigned to each arm, primary tones that could combine to make any shade on the color wheel. Blondie said with pride, "The Plexiglas separates the customer from the compressor's noise and the fumes."

"Whoa yeah," Ace breathed.

"I like the Sensory Deprivation chamber," Big Guns divulged.

Shocker nodded to him. "I tried one during a training camp in Colorado. I was blinded with black goggles, ears and nose plugged, while I floated in a tank of water. There was no sensation to distract me. I could do complicated math problems in my head." She looked wistful. "Ugh, I wish I had one at home. Thirty minutes in that thing and I felt like I slept all night."

Big Guns laughed. "Same with me. I could think clearer, deeper and," silver grunt, " 'paint.' I can't draw a stick man on paper –"

"No problem drawing bombs, though," Blondie muttered, then smiled at him to continue.

"Yeah. I said I was sorry about that." He glanced at me. I shrugged, *Between you and her, pal. I was okay with what happened.* He mumbled a curse, then turned back to Shocker. "With her machine I can paint abstract scenes that actually look good."

"Clarice taught me how to paint on canvas," Bobby told us, looking at Shocker. He told her, "Boss, you said robots would take over everything."

"I meant car manufacturing," she said in wonder. Looked at Blondie. "How does it know what to paint?"

"Again, it's a reverse Rorschach concept." She walked into the room, ran a hand over the recliner's headrest. "If you look at a triangle, for example, your brain emits a specific electrical signature. Colors do the same thing: red revs the libido or evokes competitiveness. Like that. There's decades of research on that stuff. Whatever you think, feel, or visualize is interpreted by software and painted on canvas by the 'bot. We have different canvases for different time limits."

l pointed at the Chapel. "People that paint their prayers use a small canvas for ten minutes."

"Most of my prayers are full of curses these days." Shocker looked dour. "Don't think I'll be using that one."

Anh Long had remained quiet during Blondie's hosting, standing behind everyone with increasingly impatient eyes. He broke his silence. "This is all very impressive, but you didn't bring us here to have us paint our muses."

"True." Blondie turned to look at the old man, her congenial spirit vanishing. Ms. All Business: "This way."

She shouldered through our group and strutted with purpose down the hallway.

Shocker frowned at the Elder Dragon before taking Ace' s hand to pull him away from his inspection of several Emotion Art paintings hanging behind the service desk. Large and small canvases were framed in titanium, each with golden plaques engraved with titles. My favorites were the huge one with twisting sprays of greens and yellows titled, "Prayer To Legalize It", and the blank white one that said, "Boyfriend's Thoughts On Marriage". A small one to the far right with broad splashes of pink was enscripted, "Child With Lollipop".

…worth their paint, my subconscious opined as I took up the rear of our train.

The back room had a steel door with a thick seal to contain all the noise produced by Blondie's inner mad scientist (who by the way, is hell on heels). It was a workshop for researching and developing EEG concepts. Two long steel tables stretched the length of the floor, both covered in electronic components, soldering and jig stations, engineering manuals (written and illustrated by Blondie) and several laptops. Boxes of chemicals and safety gear were stored on shelves on the back wall, a sandblasting machine and 3D printer in either corner. My girl did some serious fabricating in this room. The smells of various consumables and new cables piqued the craftsman in Ace, Shocker and Bobby. They peered around at the specialty tools and diagnostic machines with unreserved delight, right at home.

"What's down there?" Ace asked, pointing to a corner junction box with electrical conduits running into the foundation. A large black rubber mat lay in front of it, hiding a door to an illegal basement.

Blondie glanced at me with a hint of irritation. I nodded, *Might as well,* and she relaxed, said, "Guess I shouldn't be surprised you noticed that." Shocker looked at her man with glowing approval. Blondie sighed and told everyone, "I don't like to show anyone my garden -"

"*Our* garden," I cut in, gaining odd looks.

"Our garden." Flip of luscious hair in my direction. "We'll take a tour after we look at the helmets."

"Helmets," Bobby said. He made a weird face, *What next?*

Big Guns looked at him. "Yeah. Doesn't sound good, right?"

"For real. When you need specialized helmets for a job you know it's gonna be a mother'." His chest and arms jumped for emphasis.

"Wire pullers," *Anh Long* said, "use secret means to influence or undermine an organization." The corner of his mouth turned up as he looked at Bobby. "It is wise for a wire puller to have proper safety gear."

Bobby frowned thoughtfully.

Anh Long turned to Blondie. "Did you make one for me, dear,?"

She smiled sweetly. "Nope."

He pretended to be hurt, holding out his hands like, *You think I'm too old for this business???* He waved both hands, *Bah!* and chuckled.

He was aware she thought him rude earlier and was attempting to ease the tension.

Blondie pointed at a machine the size of a large deep freezer. "Additive manufacturing. Took about twenty hours to print each helmet."

"Three-D printing." Shocker walked over to the machine. "I've read about these but haven't seen one yet."

"That model can print anything," Ace stated next to her. "It can use plastic polymers or metals in liquid or powder form. An electron beam melts the particles in a pattern dictated by a CAD file." He gestured with his long arms. "The machine's rake distributes a fine layer of material across the build platform. The platform lowers slightly and the process repeats until the object has been fully printed."

"CAD?" Big Guns was acutely interested.

"Computer-aided design," the geek supplied. "Allows engineers to tweak the design on a computer before building begins. Saves a lot of R and D time. And money."

Big Guns' inner gangster bloomed on his wide face, exuding criminal swag. In a voice loaded with illicit intent he asked, "Can it print guns?"

The Viet underboss was known for customizing .45 Smith & Wessons, and had a nearly daily habit of sketching ordinance of his own design on whatever scraps of paper he randomly found. The crazy bastard was wide open with it at times. Once he drew an ammonium nitrate bomb on a napkin while we were eating with Blondie and Trinh at a trendy restaurant. The waiter saw it, peered curiously at it, and froze with recognition. His Hello-My-Name-Is-Mark face took one look at the bomb artist's intense, gangster eyes, and turned around and proceeded to the nearest phone to call the police.

"MFer," Blondie scolded Big Guns, throwing her napkin in his face before we hurriedly left the restaurant. Trinh put him on kitty cat restriction, and Blondie was pissed the evening was ruined. I, on the other hand, saw the plus side: we didn't have to pay for the meal we nearly finished!

Blondie looked at Big Guns and said flatly, "We are not going to start a gun factory."

"Not 'we'." Silver flash. "*I*. With my own machine I'll be purchasing soon."

She narrowed her green gaze for a moment more. "Then yeah. This model will print the individual parts. You'll have to use a micrometer to check the specs and do a little slag filing. Then assemble the parts."

His face split into a grin that made his teeth emit chromatic flares. The man was experiencing a life changing moment. He ran a hand over the viewing glass on the front of the printer. "I want to see my helmet."

"Me too." Shocker wore an enthusiastic glow too, though hers was more of a teenager in a shopping mall that couldn't wait to try on the latest fashion accessories.

Large steel cabinets flanked the 3D printer. I watched Blondie's glutes as she sashayed a few steps over and opened the one on the right. Inside, full-faced motorcycle-style helmets, jet black, were positioned in rows on the top two shelves, each almost imperceptibly different in size. She grabbed the largest one and handed it to Bobby. He grinned, accepting it. She handed out the rest and we tried them on.

"Carbon fiber and Kevlar composite." Ace's voice was muffled until he opened the clear face shield. He tapped the side of the helmet. "Bulletproof, to a very high degree." He shook his head, hard. "Nice fit."

Blondie beamed at the materials scientist, then walked around the back of everyone, flicking a small toggle inside the helmets by the neck. She turned to face us, pushed and held a button under the chin of her helmet. She took a breath and pressed her lips together in concentration. In the helmets we heard a robot Blondie say, "Good to go."

Big Guns' helmet jerked back as if to avoid a punch. He stared at her incredulously. "*Cac!* What the hell was that?!" Everyone else looked just as startled. He continued staring, blinking, comically confused in his Star Trek headgear. He knew her lips hadn't moved.

"Covert op tech for now," I said, enjoying their reaction to my girl's masterpiece. "Though in a few years it might be Big Brother in your head."

"I'm blown away," Shocker said, looking at the Elder Dragon. The old dude crossed his arms, patience challenged. He wanted to try on a helmet.

"Did you get this from DARPA?" Ace muttered, then answered himself. "No, couldn't have."

The girl-beast peered through her face shield at Ace. "Defense Advanced Research whatever?"

"Projects. Yeah. They are developing this tech for the intelligence community. It's potentially an evil tool. Literally a mind reading device. Government special operations teams use these in the field to help them pick friends from enemies among captured people."

"Sounds like something you'd see on SyFy," Bobby rumbled.

"Yesterday's science fiction is today's reality," I felt I had to say. Then commented to Bobby, "That futuristic helmet makes your muscle-towered ass look like a super ninja action figure."

"Super Nigga," he replied, nodding. He gripped his hands behind his back, executing a triceps pose.

Shocker chimed in with a burst of squealing humor. "Blondie could make little Bobby figures with the three-D printer." She gave her friend a teasing look that made him step into an impressive chest flexing pose. She squeezed his heavily muscled arm. "Every kid would want to chew on it and smash it."

The room reverberated laughter. Bobby took off his helmet and shook his head at her, *That's just wrong, Boss.* He was too dark to show a blush but we all knew he was.

Blondie refocused the group. "Veritas Scientific started developing this technology about seven years ago. Their designs aren't public so I couldn't copy their work. But I knew it was possible. I just had to figure it out myself, while perfecting the Emotion Art concept." She glanced at me. "We wanted to be able to communicate on jobs without talking out loud."

Nodded in her direction. "Her sign language sucks. It's like she has four middle fingers."

Ace frowned at her. "Does everyone hear your voice?"

She shrugged sheepishly. "Haven't had the chance to write new software. My helmet transmits his voice." She pointed at me with her middle finger.

Big Guns pushed his transmit button. "This will be useful..." Blondie's computer monotone said. He spoke out loud. "How many words can it pick up?"

Blondie took her's off. Everyone followed suit and she lectured, "The EEG measures brain activity with electrodes lining the helmet. They pick up specific words. So far I've managed to find about four hundred words. And it took a year and hundreds of cortex scans to recognize that much. The helmet can also be used as a lie detector." For some reason she looked at me. "I had a great subject to calibrate that function on."

My voice adopted a boasting inflection. I pointed at myself. "Great subject."

"Accomplished liar, you mean," Shocker pooh-poohed me.

"*Great subject*," I argued.

"Con artist."

"Great. Subject."

"Scammer."

"GreatsubjectgreatsubjectgreatsubjectGREATSUBJECT!"

"Shut up."

"You shut up."

We grinned hugely at each other.

"Children, please." Blondie flipped her hair primly, then muttered, "I need a doob."

I leapt away from the group, landed, flicked my right boot over my left and scissored my legs, executing a tight, fast spin. "Stop! Doobie time." The notion of seeing and smelling our little paradise of herb and fungus always made me feel like dancing. Antsy as a chubby kid listening to the ice cream man approach, I moonwalked to the corner until I hit the black mat. Squatted down and plucked it up with a flourish, rolled it over, revealing the steel bunker door underneath. Next to it in a small relief was a combination key pad and T-handle. I turned my back to everyone and entered the code: UNLAWFUL.

"Awful and unlawful we are," I said in my Yoda voice. "*Criminal Jedi.*"

Turning the T-handle had two jobs: unlocking the door and triggering a relay for the lights. The weather seal hissed slightly as the cool dry air of the building mixed with the warm humidity in the basement, energy saving LEDs illuminating the seven foot shaft and steel ladder. Without an invitation or so much as a glance at anyone I jumped into the hole with arms stretched over my head, foregoing the ladder completely.

"*Weeee!*" my giddy, dumb ass said during the drop.

My injured calf was not in agreement with the landing. The nerves voiced a searing curse that radiated up the back of my leg for several very long seconds. Fortunately, Ace's compression legging absorbed some of the impact.

That, my subconscious said with a phantom grimace, *was REALLY dumb.*

I rubbed my leg, holding my breath. "Yep," I gasped.

I watched Blondie's legs and crotch as she climbed down, her curves and crevices renewing the elation, dampening the pain. Still rubbing my calf I told her, "The sight of you is narcotic."

She dusted off hands that had no dust on them. Looked at my leg and sighed, *Idiot,* though my compliment put a pleased shine in her eyes.

The others climbed down and followed us into the twenty foot circular room of unlawfulness.

"So this is where the legendary Fairy Dust comes from," Big Guns said in accusation. "Fairy Dust" is what Blondie's exclusive, extremely fortunate clientele called her weed. He grunted. "*Du ma,* you bubble gum pop trailer trash princess. You suck." His eyes and teeth dazzled with mock hurt. He took his phone out. "I'm unfriending you."

"Shut up." She tagged his meaty shoulder with a stiff jab, smiling at his grunt. "*Lon.* You need to stop watching romantic comedies with Trinh. You've become as sensitive as a sitcom homo."

His mouth twisted around as if he were struggling to swallow something unpleasant, holding back an outburst that would only strengthen her roast.

"Ha!" I pointed and laughed. "Thespian *Ion*."

"Razor…" he growled in warning. Everyone smiling at him wasn't helping. I knew how he felt. Blondie did that to me in front of people all the time. Never get used to it.

It's that magazine's fault, I thought. *Damn* Psychology Today.

With a rare show of sympathy I dropped the banter. "Sorry. I'm sober." I grinned at the room. "But not for long. Check out the setup."

Gray concrete absorbed the dim shaded grow lights hovering over head-high plants of marijuana, each potted inside its own glass incubator on black stools. Hoses and wires ran up the stool legs, irrigation and day/night hardware that allowed the operation to run nearly autonomously.

As their mystified minds took it all in a small pump on the floor hummed to life. A light mist began to fog the glass of the two dozen incubators, softly glowing clouds enveloping the leafy budding plants, wet tickling caresses. *Yummy.* I shivered in delight. Goosebumps zinged up my arms, chest and face. I stepped out a simple jazz dance, rolling my fists, a youngster in Willy Wonka's chocolate factory.

The pump clicked off. Everyone stood transfixed, the only sound a soft moan from the ventilation system, sophisticated filtration of the moist, pungent air. I became aware of Blondie studying the plants, taking deep, satisfied, boobies-poking-out breaths. Her pride in her work and her intent to sample the fruit was stronger than mine.

"Whoa. Is that set to Rainforest, or what?" Ace asked, squinting a smile, walking down a row of misty incubators.

Blondie followed him. "Fairy Forest," she replied.

"Boss, you like mushrooms." Bobby's basso swelled the room with good nature. He suggested, "Chop up one of those little devils to eat with your steak."

"Pfff," she responded.

Her and Bobby had walked to the end of the incubators and stood looking at two enormous aquariums mounted on the back wall. The one hundred gallon tanks were lined with several inches of cow manure, dark with moisture, warm, capped with humidifiers and heaters for ideal fungi growing conditions. Shocker wagged her ponytail. "Where's the caterpillar smoking the water bong?" She wanted to know.

"Take one of those and find out," I told her, stepping over to a desk and grabbing a bottle of pills. Poured a few in my palm. The purple gel caps were filled with concentrated psilocybin, the active ingredient in "magic" mushrooms. I cultivate and process it for occasional recreation use, though my primary purpose was actually a research project. There are a lot of other uses for the stuff, real science that is interesting and helpful. Plus, I get really bored and feel like playing with drugs. I told the girl-beast, "These will help your temper." As smoothly, innocently, as I could I added, "Maybe permanently."

She wasn't going for it. Hands on hips, she eyed me skeptically and said, "Pass." She turned back to the tanks, mushrooms sprouting out of moo turds, and twisted her jaw, grossed out. "They're *slimy*. Ew."

"I thought you were full of it. *Du ma*." Big Guns laughed. He looked at the pills in my hand. "You really made shroom pills. Have you convinced anyone cooking their mind with false reality will solve all their problems?" Grunt. "I'll say it again: I think you just like fucking with people."

I smirked, *Maybe*. Looked at the tanks. The dung had brown nippled pale caps, large and small, sticking up in all directions from slim stems with delicate purple skirts. Thick mucus shined on the tips of my fungal flora. I felt a slight irritation at not being taken seriously, and looked at my Viet counterpart with affected patience. "Personality shifts tend to be slow and gradual. A person can go to therapy for years and never achieve the change they seek. A single dose of psilocybin can do it in twelve hours, and make a long-lasting or even permanent change in a person's sense of wellbeing and life satisfaction. People become more creative and in touch with reality because they are humbled by nature's immensity during the trip."

Ace fidgeted to add something. I nodded, *Go ahead,* and he let out a breath. Said, "Steve Jobs credits his LSD experiences as the most profound and creativity-enhancing of his life. If not for psychedelic drugs, we wouldn't have iPhones, iPods, or iPads."

"Really?" Shocker had a hand on her pocket, squeezing her iPhone. She looked less disgusted, though reluctantly so.

Ace squinted in recollection. "When I first read that I wanted to try it, see what ideas followed." He looked down and half mumbled, "But in those days I was so wired-in I couldn't stand to leave my screen, much less actually leave the apartment to hunt drugs."

Blondie put a hand to her mouth, laughing at him. She could certainly relate. I can recall many times when she got strung out on hacking adventures and I had to play Dr. Phil to talk her away from the laptop. I recall eating a few punches, too.

I stuck a handful of pills in my pocket, set the bottle down and said, "Psychedelics can induce a positive personality change instantly. There's never been anything else that can do that."

"That is dramatic," *Anh Long* said with one thick brow lifted, his earlier impatience gone; he had warmed to our unique science projects. He grinned with hooded eyes and said, "I took mushrooms in Vietnam as a young man. There were eccentric groups of monks that used them for spiritual journeys, and of course we young villagers just had to try it. I remember a gathering where everyone was so happy and carefree. It confused and angered me. What was there to celebrate? I was so focused on the mundane details and the endless suffering that I couldn't understand. Then later that evening I went with a group to some temple ruins that were a thousand years old. We drank some awful tea." He smiled at the memory.

Blondie, Big Guns, and myself - the only other people present who have experienced that awful taste - laughed and encouraged him to go on.

"After the tea took effect, those ancient ruins became another reality. It was reality *shattering*. The temples and stone courtyards where men lived, prayed and fought for their lives were windows to another world. I recall thinking very clearly: I am a speck of dust in time. That place was a thousand years old, the people and their problems long gone, and no one remembers them or cares. Their struggles were insignificant in the big picture, and so are mine. It was ego loss. I wasn't a proud young Vietnamese fisherman trying to make a life. The hallucinations made me see there is something that is me that has nothing to do with that and is far, far more important." Another nostalgic smile. "And far more significant."

"Deep," Bobby said. He studied the mushrooms. "So I could get my spirit on and maybe hallucinate something I'd want to paint later." Scratched his head. "What else do they do?"

"Most drugs only work while you take them," I informed my potential research subject. "Psychedelics clear the body within hours, but the effects can last a lifetime. I think current research will lead to treatments for depression."

"We could use that in Mississippi," *Anh Long* said a tad woefully. "Everyone is obese and depressed about it."

"Is it like Prozac?" Shocker queried.

Smiling at the thought of the entire state on my pills, I explained to her, "Better. People who get into depressive thinking have over-connected brains. Regret and self-criticism creates repetitive background chatter. Psilocybin dampens the circuits to the sense of self."

"Ego loss," *Anh Long* said with a nod.

"Right. That allows people to escape from being tethered to that particular thinking process."

"Psilocybin mimics serotonin, the brain chemical responsible for regulating mood," Ace said. The added to himself, "Most antidepressants target serotonin...*fascinating*."

"Lacking feelings of love or connectedness with your wife?" I asked Big Swoll with a stupid grin. "It recalibrates how people experience consciousness. After a trip people commonly resolve to be more in the moment. You will appreciate your woman far more."

Blondie laughed supportively. Rubbed my arm and said to them, "Fucker even helps with the laundry after a trip." She gestured after everyone laughed. "But unfortunately that's not a permanent change to his personality."

My hands decided it was a good time to twist some pubbies. I stepped behind her, pulled her tightly to me and pinched the front of her dress and the blonde sunflowers underneath. Turned them sharply, then let go, all too quickly for anyone to have noticed.

She gasped and squirmed, cut her eyes reprovingly as she broke loose and shoved me away. She glared, *Not in front of company!*

But she likes it, I knew with confidence.

Feeling like I had been exposed to the drug I was promoting, I turned back to Bobby with a question on my face.

"Uh..." he hedged.

"Pass," Shocker told him sternly.

Quick glance at her. He sighed, "Pass."

Blondie rolled her eyes, *Whatev'*. She took the bottle of pills and offered it to *Anh Long*. He grinned and helped himself, poured out a few and pocketed them.

I wonder if he'll agree to carry a camcorder during his adventure...

"*Cac.*" Big Guns swore while looking at his phone. "No reception down here. I have to go up." Silver trepidation emitted between his lips. "I'm surprised Gat hasn't come to see why I'm not answering reports."

Anh Long turned to follow his *Em Hung* up the ladder. "We'll be at the coffee bar."

"We'll come with you guys." Shocker looked relieved to have a reason to leave our garden of evil. She took her man's arm and pulled him after her, his face burning with unfinished intellectual stimulation. He turned away from the shroom tanks and incubators with a sigh, followed his stern-faced wife.

Blondie clearly wanted to continue her hosting role, but also wanted to grab some Fairy Dust. She began to dart to the desk but I waved for her to stop. "I'll get the Dust. You handle the social intercourse."

Smiling, *Thanks,* she rushed after our guests and left me to do a little herb shopping. A mouth-watering arrangement of Mason jars completely absorbed my attention. Above the desk were three shelves, each one containing different strains of bunched, sticky, multi-shades of green, slap-yo-grandmammy buds of marijuana. "Hello there," I greeted them.

I picked up a jar with a sticker on the front depicting a tiny blonde fairy waving a wand, magical sparkles issuing from it. Opened it with my muzzle stuck to the lid, inhaling like a fourteen year old huffing Whiteout. The anticipation built quickly. I serenaded the drug. "I want to smoke you like an animal…"

A drawer in the desk provided a box of Ziploc baggies. As I started to bag my groceries a faint *pop* snagged my attention. I froze, listening hard, paranoia creeping in, hoping some hooptie had backfired when, *Pop! Pop!* BOOM! BOOM! more gunshots erupted from the parking lot, shattering the boutique's front glass next door, subsequent shots heard louder through the opening.

Someone is moving on us!

"Blondie…"

I don't remember dropping the jar or climbing the ladder. A blur of movement brought me to the hallway door adjoining the two businesses. It was open, Shocker's and Ace's legs sticking out on this side as they lay on the floor with arms over heads. Bullets rained into the boutique's front room with piercing cracks, rips, and thuds, shredding merchandise into debris that flew like shrapnel into the hall, bits of jackets, purses and lingerie cascading down on top of the girl-beast and geek. Crystal's slasher flick screams filled the short pauses between bursts, Blondie yelling over the discord for everyone to get behind the bar.

Thick oak with a granite top. Good thinking, I praised my blonde warrior. Then, *She won't leave Crystal. We'll have to escape out the back, using something to shield... But what?*

"Challenge," I said, inhaling deeply as my good buddy Adrenaline surged through my chest and limbs with tidal force. "This should be fun."

"Hey asshole." Shocker glared up at me, then flinched as more rounds tore through the thin panels and frame just above her. "Quit stroking your death wish and figure out how we can get out of this."

"Simple," I replied with a wolfish baring of teeth. "Our pack has to out maneuver theirs." I crouched down, acutely aware of the intensity radiating from them as I visualized what we must do. "You two get the helmets. There are six suits in the cabinet next to it. Grab those and meet me at the bar. We'll make our play for the ally." I waited for a pause in the barrage and stepped over them quickly, sprinting into the fray, hoping my skull and organs followed me into the next room.

She yelled after me, "Helmets and suits?! Where are the freaking weapons???"

I dove and slid on my stomach right as more bullets slammed into the hallway. Crashed into a stool. Scrambled around the bar like a dog clawing on tile with no traction. Bobby lay over Crystal like a grizzly rug, Blondie and the Viet men hunkered down in front of them. Big Guns hefted twin chrome .45s with a thoroughly pissed off face eyeing me between them. "Gat?" I asked him.

He snarled, "Him and others. They flipped on me!" His face was thunderous. "Those I know are still loyal aren't answering. And no one is answering at the garage either."

Bad. It's all bad. That's all of his top men!

Tho and carl...

I tried to project calm command. "They have maybe five minutes before Biloxi PD shows up. More or less. They'll move in quickly, front and back."

"Duh," Shocker said behind me, sliding in with Ace. They dumped arms full of helmets and black riding suits on the floor. "You said we're going out the back. These bulletproof?"

"Sort of," Blondie answered.

"Close enough." I grabbed my suit from the pile and kicked off my boots, quickly standing and stepping into it. Zipped up the front. With jeans on the tight suit was incredibly ball-smashing.

Well fuck you, too! they burned as I slipped my boots back on.

"Service ally," I groaned. "There are several Dumpsters we can use for cover."

"Those rifles would shred a car," Big Guns said, nodding. He looked at *Anh Long,* his liege he had sworn to protect. He spoke to him in Vietnamese, asking if my plan was acceptable.

The old man grabbed Big Guns' shoulder. "I trust your judgement, *Em Hung.*"

Big Guns met my eyes, waved a gun, *Let's do it, bro.*

"I'm assuming these are ours." Shocker indicated the suits, then impatiently handed my helmet to me. Blondie pointed out who got what and everyone tugged on their outfits in a frenzy.

The assault became sporadic shots, then ceased altogether. Without the deafening destruction we could hear faint yells from shoppers around the plaza, their vehicles racing away. Closer to the boutique we listened to the commands from our enemy barked in harsh, foreign dialect. And in the bar we heard our hearts pounding. I put my helmet on. "Gloves," I complained to Blondie, looking at my hands. "We forgot gloves. Can you make these play music?" I tapped the helmet.

"You're going to hear a lively drum solo if you don't tell me exactly what you're going to do," she said, eyes full of worry despite her querulous tone. Her dress and heels on the floor, she zipped up her suit and moved to take Crystal's sandals, slipped them on.

"I'll go over the roof and drop down on the first targets I find. Phong will send the cannon fodder first, not his best." I pointed at Big Guns. "Go out the front of Emotion Art. There's a concrete pillar by the entrance. I'll meet you there."

Got it, he grunted.

Big Guns stood to go. Shocker grabbed him. "Give me one." He handed her a gun. She eyed it like a veteran marksman, then looked at me and said, "I'll cover you."

Blondie made sure everyone had their helmets turned on, *Anh Long* and Crystal the only ones without. She told me, "You're going for the Bronco, aren't you."

I grinned in answer, then turned to the geek. "Ace, they'll chase us around back. When they do make a break for your car. Meet us at the end of the building. Get *Anh Long* and Crystal out of the Dumpster. Hide them."

"I can do that," he said. He licked his lips nervously and closed his face shield.

Anh Long sighed heavily. Crystal's eyes widened. She moaned, "Dumpster? You're putting me in *garbage???*" She began to sob. Bobby rubbed her back in a soothing gesture.

Shoes crunched glass in the front room. Big Guns was on point, already moving through the hall. He ducked through the door to Emotion Art, then swung back out a moment later and dropped a tall, slim Asian thug creeping over the front desk, coming in the busted window with an SKS aimed at the hall. Big Guns' .45 roared once, incredibly loud in the small space. The target tumbled to the floor in serious pain. The sound wave hadn't fully dissipated before I yelled "Go!" and began shoving everyone into the tiny room behind the bar, lining them up between two tables holding eight Draganflies. We heard Big Guns' arrival out front, gun blazing, giving our enemies second thoughts about sending anyone else in from that direction.

How many are out there? I wondered. *Out back?*

EXIT was stenciled on the black steel service door. I hit the push bar, opening it, ducking. Bullets immediately pelted it from both sides, ricocheting wildly before the door slammed shut.

"Ooh, good plan Mister President," Shocker said, crouched like a leather encased spring of muscle next to me. She smacked my shoulder.

"You do realize this is going to sting like a biatch, right? I've seen better planning form my twelve year old son."

I looked at her. "I didn't say it was a plan." I steeled myself, preparing to sprint out into the hail of bullets. "I said it was a *challenge.*"

I swung the door, flung myself out and to the right, cringing furiously as my sack flared ungodly pain. "Not a running suit," I breathed. A slug hit me in the left shoulder pad as four gangsters stood from behind wooden pallets and tried to murder me. I stumbled at the numbing blow, started zigzagging. Shocker screamed behind me, door crashing open, and let loose, the Smith & Wesson booming potential death at the ducking, cursing enemy. She dipped back inside, their shots thudding into the door she just barely closed in time.

Fifty yards away I leapt into an open Dumpster, crushing office trash, happy it wasn't refuse from the deli. I wallowed around in the sluggish mess, wincing as someone emptied their clip into my hiding place, thick steel sides buzzing my helmet with concussions that blurred my vision intensely. The assault stopped, and I sensed my attackers were attempting to get in better position to shoot inside the Dumpster.

"Lovely," I growled. Pain began to throb in my shoulder as the numbness wore off. Luckily the round hadn't penetrated. The motorcycle racing suit had layers of leather and carbon fiber to protect skin from asphalt at high speeds. Blondie's addition of a Kevlar layer made the suits resistant to small arms fire, with thick pads that could stop rifle rounds, though they were by no means bruise resistant.

Four years ago we needed these suits for a job we knew would get us shot. It did. Her suits protected us, excepting a fractured metacarpal I sustained as slugs rearranged 'Zuki's face and crushed my left hand. Kevlar pads were inserted in the forearms, elbows, shoulders, chest and back as extra protection. Ditto the legs. *Still no gloves,* my hand ached.

"Dummy," Robot Blondie said in my helmet. Then, "You there... you okay...."

I pressed the transmit button under the chin and thought-sent, *Okay... going to push the... front of the door... hook... to the truck... I drive around...*

"Okay."

I climbed over the side quickly, but not quicker than the round that found my helmet as the killers opened up. The SKS projectile rammed into my helmet, head darting to the side unexpectedly, tearing something in my neck that burned alarmingly. I couldn't stop myself from collapsing, body following head to the ground. Gritting my teeth, I tried to make my eyes focus. That shit *hurt.* "Uh. Ow." I felt the side of the helmet. It wasn't a glancing blow. It was a direct hit, a small section flaked away, though it wasn't cracked. The street and building in sharp focus again, I got my feet under me, muttering, "Now I know what a punch from George Foreman feels like."

Shots rang from over the roof. People were still screaming and racing out of the plaza. I grinned. Big Guns was giving them fits. He was a master of urban warfare, having been in gang battles - having *trained* for gang battles - all his life. So I wasn't worried about him.

Clock was ticking to the ring of his emptying clips. I had to get into position before he ran out.

"I have three...left..." Robot Blondie informed the team.

That's Shocker, I realized. Weird. I sent, *Okay... going over now...* and wondered how strange it was for her to hear Blondie's voice coming from me.

The four Viet gangsters had turned into six. As I studied their bold walks with no cover I was sure they were 211 and OBG, not Diep's elite boys. But that didn't mean they lacked for hardware and ammunition. The pavement on both sides of the Dumpster spat rocks as a renewed assault pockmarked the surface, 7.62mm slugs rebounding off the building, into the lot of the lawn and garden store on the other side of the chain-link fence. They were trying to pin me down, keep me in this spot so they could get close enough for clear shots.

A child's frightened, excited squeal made me look left, at the nail salon. Someone had cracked open the service exit. Huddled by the gap were two girls younger than ten, and a boy of about fifteen stood behind them. Kids of the owners, a Mexican couple that did great nails and were teaching the trade to their progeny. They must have gone to lunch, leaving the eldest to sit the girls.

I looked at the boy, opened my face shield and shouted, "What's wrong with you, kid?! Get back inside!" I pointed harshly and he slowly closed the door. "Goddamn *kids.*" I slammed the face shield.

Beside each of the eight doors were large pipes that drained water from the roof gutters. Next to the pipes were sections of concrete ribs that stuck out to support the building's structure. I darted behind the nearest one, spray of bullets following, pinging away chunks of the pavement and rib, wall. I looked up. The roof was only twelve feet, though it looked like Mount Everest at this point in my fun filled day.

I grabbed the pipe, stuck a boot on the rib, the other on the wall, and pushed hard, pulling with my arms. My shoulder protested, but I went up easily enough, hand over hand, baby walking quickly. My helmet broached the summit, sighting the flat roof topped with bright white paint. Put one arm over to pull myself up-

And half a dozen slugs tore into the Kevlar pads in my back, knocking me around spasmodically, dislodging my grip. "Mother-*fuck,*" I gasped as that tramp Gravity snatched me back to the pavement.

My boots, butt, back and helmet hit in split-second succession, ankles, knees and injured calf tingle-burning with trauma. I managed not to waste time yelling, rolled in time to gain cover behind my big blue pal once more. Their rifle fire peppered the Dumpster. A ricochet came off the building wall and hit me in the side. It knocked dust from my ass and wind from my lungs.

Diaphragm locked up, lungs refusing to work, black swirls invaded my helmet, and my hearing dulled severely. Distantly I heard Shocker's crazed battle cry and her remaining bullets boom before the boutique's door crashed shut, return fire thundering into it.

"Razor," Robot Blondie said amidst black swirls. "You okay…you take too long."

"Stop nagging," I hiccupped painfully. I pressed the send button. "*Okay... hang on...*" Groaned and got up. "Nag, nag, nag. Always when I take too long. *I like the exclamation point better*," I mimicked my girl. "*The sunflowers took too long.*" I winced out a breath. "I'll nag her blonde pubbies for that."

I looked left, moved and took a quick glance around. Two Asian dudes that didn't look old enough to drink yet crept along the fence, one behind the other, SKSs held in wary hands. The thug in the lead reached back and pulled up his sagging pants, then waved for his associate to go around the other side of my hiding place so they could encircle me.

I looked up and cursed the Odds. "Bitch." Then took off my helmet, the only thing I had to use as a weapon. Another glance. Right as they began to part I jumped out and slung the helmet at them as hard as I could, a roaring big alpha wolf, running in to rip and shred my prey.

They jerked their guns up and fired, aim way off because their eyes were distracted by the large black projectile coming at them. The helmet *thunked* into the face of the one in the rear, a single bullet nicking my arm before I closed the distance. "GET SOME!" I bellowed, propelling all my speed and weight behind a straight-right that hit the lead guy so hard his ancestors overseas felt it. Skin smacked open, eye orbit crumbling under my knuckles. He spun sideways into his buddy and collapsed, unperceiving head hitting the ground with a wet, hollow, dropped-melon *thud.*

Without stopping to pose I kept the momentum flowing and lunged at the second target, slapping aside the barrel of his rifle as he fired point blank at my stomach. The round took a plug of leather out of the suit, scoring a white hot trench across my abs. A right-hand, left-hook flashed and ended any thoughts he had of stopping me.

I had an urge to drop down on all fours and feast on my prey, teeth bared, slavering. I resisted it, dropping down instead to grab a rifle, having just enough time to throw myself behind a rib on the building. The remaining four gangsters emptied fresh clips at my back as soon as I moved away from their wounded comrades.

A round that hit inches from my leg sprayed me with fine particles of concrete, deflecting and sinking into the gut of the first guy I had punched. A portion of his consciousness had awakened, instinct making him moan a high-pitched wounded animal noise that conjured terrible feelings in my stomach, spreading to wobble my legs. I didn't mind hurting idiots like him, but the depth of suffering he just voiced was on a level I had no intention of inflicting.

Someone shouted, "*Ngung!*" stop, and the fusillade ceased, cracking echoes fading toward the distant police sirens.

I still have time, I hoped. I had a rifle. These ignoramuses won't approach me so boldly now. I glanced at the nail salon. The door was open again. Perfect. The same curious faces peered out with their too big eyes. I shook my head, slid along the wall, and glared at the boy. "*¡Estupido muchacho!*" stupid kid. "You trying to get your *hermanas* hurt?"

He shook his head, slowly closed the door.

I waved frantically. "Wait! *Esperas y veras.*"

He eased the door back open.

I said, "Will you help me?"

He shook his head.

I smiled a little. "I'll give you a hundred dollars."

He matched my smirk of greed. He nodded.

I patted my pockets, realizing my cash was in my jeans, no time to dig it out. I said, "I can pay you later. I'm good for it."

His black hair shook. His large eyes darkened as the door slowly closed.

"*¡Espera!* Hold on, *muchacho.*" I looked around, saw the enemy were still behind the stack of pallets, looked at the unconscious thugs, at the gun lying next to them. I told the boy, "You see that SKS?"

Yes, he nodded with keen interest.

"You can have it, and any cash they have on them. Grab it when they chase me."

He gave me an exasperated look, *That was going to be mine, anyway.* Then he shrugged and nodded.

"I'd make a good dad," I muttered. "My ass."

The rifle had a shoulder strap. I slung it over my head and arm, then had the boy give me a boost, boot pushing off his interlaced hands, climbing on top of the door. As soon as I was up the goons fired at me again. "Inside *muchachos*!" I yelled, stretching and pulling myself onto the roof, rolling away from the edge.

Without the helmet I couldn't know the status of my crew. The shout in Vietnamese to shoot the boutique door's lock and the sudden increase in iron hail out front told me all I needed, however. "I'm taking too long," I nagged myself.

Standing, I sprinted to the front, ducked down next to a huge heat pump, the square of metal covering me while allowing a view of the parking lot. Men crouched between rows of cars, guns over fenders and roofs. I sensed they weren't very enthusiastic about going through the notorious Big Guns to get inside. His reputation was holding them at bay as much as his chrome .45.

I pulled the SKS over my head, dark wooden stock warm and oily, shouldered it and sighted through the small scope while propping the weapon on its 30-round clip. The crosshairs centered on a target about to break cover of the parked cars and rush the pillar my friend hid behind. The thug was magnified 10X, black hair sweating with anxiety in the cool air. He had protruding cheekbones and a clearly defined grim, cruel mouth. I sighted on his arm that held a large pistol. Squeezed the trigger gently…

The rifle bucked with a sharp explosion, the bullet flew true, striking the target as if an 800lb. Himalayan mountain goat had kicked him into the Nissan he crumpled against, pistol clattering, sliding under the car. He shouted like it really hurt, holding a busted arm tightly to his chest.

His brothers called out to him in panicked Vietnamese, getting wails of anguish in response. It's been a while since I've shot a rifle. I used to have one just like this. "Hmm," I said thoughtfully, looking through the scope at my work. "Like shooting the branches off a tree."

I swung the barrel to the right, spotting Phong, the 211 leader and Tiger Society underboss. His square jaw was stuck over the trunk of a sedan, angry slitted eyes directed right at me. From his relatively safe position he snapped orders to the men in the very front, near the street. One of them argued with his boss momentarily, but was quickly shamed into following two others that rushed the sidewalk while their brothers provided cover fire.

Thwack-thwack-thwack-thwack! Bullets thundered into the heat pump inches from my head, thick, supersonic, kinetic death.

"DamndamndamnFUCK!" I yelled, voice lost in the dissonance, crawling backwards before any slugs penetrated. Slid quickly to get behind another pump, mind racing.

I knew Big Guns was close to zero on ammo, and wouldn't leave his spot as long as our people were inside. Knowing I had to get on the ground and help him, this instant, I did the only thing I could do.

I stood and leapt off the roof with a Tarzan yell.

Boots-butt-back-head. That shit hurt much worse without a helmet. "Uh. *Ow.*" I scrambled to my feet.

The ape man jump had stunned our opposition long enough to roll upright and fire wild shots in their direction. Windows and headlights burst, hoods spouted holes loudly. The trio of cannon fodder abruptly had a change of heart, spinning with scared shrieks and lurching back to the parking slots.

"*Du ma!* Bout time, you round-eyed bastard," Big Guns said as I lunged onto the sidewalk, ducked next to him behind the wide pillar. He took the rifle. Detached the magazine and hefted it in his thick, stubby hand, unable to see how many rounds were left. "Sixteen," he grunted.

I groaned as awareness came to my injuries. Tapped my feet to make them quit tingling so painfully. *Two twelve foot drops back to back...* Man. There goes half the cartilage in my legs.

With an ugly grimace I looked over to the other building in the plaza, to the spot I had to run to in what I knew would be eighty yards of testicle smashing joy. I showed my friend eyes bugging with dread.

"What?" He reattached the clip.

I sighed. "The good news is Blondie won't be able to make me give her a kid after this."

"Huh?"

"Nevermind." I pointed. "I'm going for Broncostein."

He looked across the parking area, at the front of the machine shop that sat at a right angle with the end of Blondie's building. A green and white '67 Ford Bronco 4x4 loomed over the vehicles around it, the knobbies on the 44" Super Swamper Boggers nearly visible from here. The windshield said "BRONCOSTEIN" in tall green letters, with decaled veins and straining neck muscles connecting to the B and N, gold electrodes sticking out. He grunted. "I thought old man Tiblier said you couldn't drive it."

"That is correct." I cracked my knuckles then said a bit defensively, "But that was when I wanted to drive it over a car. Like Big Foot. And Tiblier's a dick, so fuck him."

Grunt, *Sure.* "I got you. *Di di!*" go.

He dropped to one knee, turned around the pillar and fired once, twice, while I tried my damnedest to burn the soles off my Rockports, sprinting down the walk, across the drive and into the parking area. Ducked below the vehicles' rooflines, trying to maintain a good speed, a Silverado and Camry taking shots from Phong and his lieutenants. Shoppers squealed and yelled caution from huddled positions in the stores. Three sets of saucer plate eyes followed me as I passed a family hiding in a Tahoe.

Broncostein's tires came up to just below my chest. I slid to a stop behind the monster truck. An ABC Auto Salvage sticker on the rear bumper suddenly dented, ricocheting a round that whined off towards Pass Road traffic. Scrambling under the jacked up Ford, I ducked around a tire, under the rear axle, popped up on the driver's side and opened the door. Pulled myself up the seven feet to the pilot's chair. Shut it, and surveyed the scene from my elevated position.

Broncostein's 460 CID big block was a work of art. Originally built for drag racing by a local junkyard king and master mechanic named K.W. Cook, the high-end engine held a special place in the heart of the machine shop owner; old man Tiblier was serious business when it came to 4-wheeling. I knew of K.W.'s work because my mentor used to race against him at Gulfport Dragway years ago. Few builders could claim to be his equal, and I felt privileged to spin this engine over.

The ignition was two toggle switches and a push button. Flick, flick, *push.* Broncostein shuddered side-to-side and came to life with a rip-snort bellow of big cam horsepower. "Fear me peasants!" I shouted, revving the beast. "Fear the Mighty Broncostein!" I gripped the wheel and shifter, depressed the clutch, excited about the potential of this rumble-snarling machine of brute power.

Police cars filled the vibrating rearview mirror as I pulled the shifter into first gear and released the clutch, flooring the gas pedal. The giant tires boiled white smoke that shrouded old man Tiblier's frantic run out of his shop to curse me.

I started to yell something about just borrowing it or maybe suggest he install a key ignition. But what came out was, "Woo-hoo, bitch!"

Second gear barked the tires as I turned into the alley behind Blondie's strip mall, huge exhaust pipes thundering off the building, heavy tire tread roaring as I weaved around the two gangsters still lying unconscious on the ground. I grinned at the absence of the SKS, but lost all humor when I looked ahead at the end of the service drive. Phong and at least ten of his crew crowded around the building with guns blazing at the cops out front. The police returned fire, shots faintly heard over Broncostein's combustion. The enemy heard me and a few turned to fire. Sparks flew from the thick steel hood, windshield blooming webs and smoking holes, ruining the graphic art.

Please don't grow a brain and shoot the tires, I grimaced.

I swerved right, ramming into a Dumpster by the fence, the roaring *boom* like a near-miss lightning strike. The Bronco's front bumper looked like it belonged on a train, an immense hunk of iron with a 4 ton wench and brush guard, barely dinging from the incredible impact, though I felt it acutely in the wheel and jarring lurch forward in the seat.

The Dumpster bounded off the fence ringing like a huge bell, spun a little and kissed the bumper again, metal grating loudly over the pavement, trailing sparks.

I floored the 460, pushing the garbage bin in front of the boutique's door, tires shielded from the barrage still coming from the enemy. Hit the brakes, massive tires shudder-barking to a stop, suspension flexing. The door burst open and a gorgeous, squealing blonde teenager flew out, arms pinwheeling, legs kicking up to show light blue panties, a modelesque arch with enough height to clear the trash.

Bobby's muscular arm flashed back inside to grab and throw package #2. *Anh Long* curled into a ball mid-air, landing on top of Crystal, who was breathless with outrage.

Blondie followed Shocker's quick crawl around the Dumpster to the front of the truck, the suits and helmets giving them confidence, while Big Guns used the door as cover to pop a few slugs at the 211 and OBG bastards that continued to shoot in seemingly all directions. Several of them jumped the fence and dove behind a selection of new riding lawn mowers.

More bullets pelted the Dumpster, rejuvenating Crystal's vocal cords. Her shrill horror ran hoarse once again when Bobby's gargantuan form came flying out the door, shadow shrouding her and *Anh Long* before his mass crushed them deep into the office trash, silencing Blondie's favorite employee.

"Haaa!" I revved Broncostein to punctuate my giddiness.

My door opened. Blondie's lithe arms stretched and strained, little hands gripping the custom handles on the rocker panel and door pillar, pulling herself up and over me to shimmy into the passenger seat. She removed the helmet, ducking golden locks below the dashboard, eyes on me, assessing injuries.

Shocker tailed her, vascular muscles snatching her into the tall vehicle like a gymnast executing a difficult move with ease. She also crawled over me, though with far less respect for placement of her elbows.

"Ffff-*uh!*" I sputtered as she clipped my chin.

"Ew," Shocker said taking off the helmet. She sat on the floorboard between the bucket seats, shifter between her legs. She looked at her elbow like she wanted to cut it off and burn it. Wiped my saliva from it.

Blondie gave her a narrow-eyed glance. Looked at me with sympathy, speaking loudly to be heard over the powerful engine. "It's hooked up, maybe three feet of slack! Go!"

"'Kay," I grunted, blinking to clear my eyes.

Reverse. I gunned the Bronco and released the clutch, whiplashing the Dumpster on the end of the winch cable, dragging the heavy steel square down the alley with an eardrum bursting grind on the pavement, racing exhaust, rifle fire and teenaged screams ringing out into the immaculate, bright blue sky.

"Woo-yeah!" my girl chortled, sitting up in the passenger seat, smoking hot in her tight black suit. "Now *this* is a truck!"

Shocker puffed irritation, though I sensed it was because she wanted to cheer as well but feared looking out of character. "Let's not celebrate until we're safe, guys!"

"Spoken like a true party pooper!" I said, watching Big Guns expend his final rounds and duck into the boutique. The Bronco's mirrors were oscillating too much to see clearly, and my ears itched maddeningly from the pressure waves of noise. I turned to look behind us, giving the 460 more fuel. "Ace out front?"

"Yeah!" Shocker answered. She stuck a finger in an ear and wiggled it. "He ran to his car when the cops chased those bozos around back!"

"Go with them!"

"No room!" she said. "Bobby, Crystal and *Anh Long* will barely fit in his car as it is!"

I glanced at her, at Blondie. "Then you get to have all the fun with us!"

She smiled in spite of herself, and my girl made an enthusiastic sound that made my jaw and crotch feel better.

Our unlikely train grind-crunch-roar-screamed to a slow at the end of the strip mall. I turned the corner, pulling the Dumpster clear of immediate danger, happy the enemy were focused on the cops for now. Hit the brakes. *And happy that Dumpster idea actually worked...*

Ace's Scion rolled up and stopped behind us. Big Swoll peered over the rim of the garbage bin, then jumped out, looking like a real Super Nigga action figure in the Kevlar suit. He turned and lifted out the Elder Dragon quickly, set him on the pavement. Grabbed Crystal and slung her over a shoulder. The girls gasped at his handling of her. I kept my lips firmly pressed together.

Anh Long didn't waste time to even look at us. He ran around the truck and climbed into the seat behind Ace, who shut his door. Bobby unhooked the cable with one hand, wrapped the short length around the brushguard. He trotted by with a bright silly grin behind the face shield, flicking a salute. We turned and watched him stuff the traumatized girl in next to *Anh Long* before sliding in front, closing the door.

"They'll have the plaza and road blocked!" Shocker screamed into her phone. "Hide behind the other building!" She nodded and ended the call.

The little sports car zipped away and turned behind the machine shop, unheard, the idling 460 continuing to rattle our auditory nerves. "Are we -" Shocker began, faltering when three Biloxi PD cruisers screeched to a stop behind us.

"Let's see what kind of suspension the old man put on this thing." I jerked it into first gear, then jumped as someone suddenly pounded his fist on my door. I looked out the window. "Hey! There he is." I glanced at the girls, jerked a thumb at the man standing by the truck.

The girls leaned over curiously. The scowling gray haired machinist continued to beat his grease stained fist on his truck, bellowing threats. Blondie frowned at him furiously. "Fuck him!"

"You goddamn outlaw scum!" Tiblier shouted. "I told you- *you can't drive it!*"

"Oh. Okay then," I told him, offering an apologetic look. "My bad."

I motioned for him to step back, like I was going to open the door. He did, hands on waist, one hell of a snarl distorting his weathered features. I gave him a thumbs up, turned to look out the windshield and revved his prized engine, launching us around the Dumpster, racing back down the service drive.

"HEEEYYY!" Tiblier's rage could be heard despite the thunderous exhaust.

Police cars suddenly turned into the drive in front of us. I didn't slow down. Shocker gripped my arm with very unfeminine force. "What are you doing?" she shouted.

To answer her question I turned right into the fence, chain-link section folding to the ground instantly, unfelt by the massive Ford, tires churning ruts up a slight slope, across the pristine lawn of the yard store we roared past, suspension abruptly jouncing us around as we whoop-dee-dooed over push mowers, weed eaters and other equipment on display, knobbies squealing traction on patios and walkways.

The lawn and garden store sat on top of a hill, with a fairly large yard and parking lot on the gentle slope. At the bottom near the road were half a dozen cars that belonged to very unlucky customers. The scene we approached made my chest freeze, like I had fallen through bayou ice, stealing my breath. Blondie growled and flipped her hair. Shocker breathed, "Oh no," staring at a stand-off right out of a J.J. Abrams film.

Multiple law enforcement agencies had Pass Road blocked, no traffic flowing, at least two dozen cruisers and a S.W.A.T. truck positioned at angles as far as I could see in either direction, surely more surrounding the block. Phong and his boys were screwed. They sat on their heels behind the customers' sedans and pickups, desperately shooting at the cops in a vain attempt to escape. S.W.A.T. knelt behind large black shields, firing M-16s with trained precision, 5.56mm slugs disintegrating the cars our enemy made their stand behind.

During our shocked pause the perpetual-scheming part of my mind finished processing the response to this situation. But before I could share it with my partners pistols cracked from right behind us, bullets thudding into the tailgate of Broncostein. The shaking mirror showed two cops in kneeling firing positions, .40 Sig Sauers aimed, shouting for us to depart the vehicle or they will fire again.

"Uh-huh," I muttered. "That's what we'll do."

I shifted into reverse and floored the beast, unleashing an enormous store of heart-palpitating torque, powering us toward the cops. They had time to fire one panicked shot before diving out of the way, narrowly avoiding the titanic Super Swampers. I turned, found first gear and launched us back toward the alley as they gained their feet and fired again, tinks and clanks faintly heard on the thick rear bumper.

"We're fucked. We're fucked!" Shocker said anxiously. She put her palms on her temples. "I'm going back to prison!"

"Not if I can help it!" I told her, barely containing a shout of joy, electrified by the challenge.

She watched me for a moment. "You're psycho!" she accused.

"That's the nicest thing you've ever said to me!"

The front-end bounced as we went over the lawn mowers again, over the fence, tires reverberating high-pitched moans onto the alley pavement. Cops covered both ends, cruisers parked nose-to-nose to block the exits. I grinned, realizing I was temporary insane, pressing the accelerator to the stop, shifting to gain speed. We rocketed down the length of the building, approaching the cop cars with the confidence of an ATV racer heading for a big jump.

It dawned on Shocker what I intended and she gripped my arm again. Blondie let out a cowgirl *yip* and grabbed the dashboard handgrip. I giggled at the cops that darted away from their cars.

WHAM!

Broncostein hit the fenders of both cruisers simultaneously, shooting straight up into the air, engine redlining as all four tires left the earth. We saw nothing but blue sky and perfect fluffy clouds for a couple of seconds and then, *SLAM!* The jarring landing rocked our senses like a slap from a bomb's shockwave. I barely held on to the wheel, foot somehow still in the throttle, feminine squawks making me smile as I downshifted to turn behind the machine shop, two black and whites on our tail a second later.

"You ramped them!" Shocker was feeling it now. "You *crushed* them!"

"You were right, Babe!" Blondie said patting the dash. "It could do it!"

Canines displayed, I caught another gear, focusing on the narrow service drive we thundered down.

Two Dumpsters were across from the machine shop and the business next to it, a small Mexican buffet with fantastic tacos. Sirens followed close behind. I glanced at the mirror, turning around as I glimpsed Ace's Scion. Debris from our wake scattered leaves and scraps of trash, momentarily outlining the invisible car parked next to Tiblier's oil recycling tank. The side of the car was projecting the street, the steel stand and cylindrical reservoir behind it, in high-definition.

"Love it!" I snickered.

The service drive ended with a wooden fence that was supposed to give the spa's sunning lounge a semblance of privacy. Broncostein crashed through it with the force of a sling blade shearing through a small twig, cracking explosively, large chunks of it flying every which way, knobbies deeply rutting grass and flower beds, crushing lawn chairs and tables vacated by fleeing, screaming, customers, plastic and metal tubes shooting out to the sides of the Ford like waves before a speeding boat.

Blink, blink, BAM! Seconds later we crashed through the other side, shards and noise terrorizing citizens that greeted us with alarmed shouts from inside their cars. We drove over the front of a Hyundai, turning into traffic on Pass Road, just outside the police barricade. The big block roared crackling thunder that crescendoed into truly powerful sound waves, dropping in pitch with every shift of gears, weaving through cars that locked up their brakes in the busy intersection, avoiding a pancaked fate.

"They can't follow!" Shocker reported, looking behind us. "The traffic is jammed!" Her smile turned uncertain when she noticed Blondie's languid posture and orgasmic expression.

Blondie opened her eyes and looked over at me, fucking me with her green gaze. She purred, "Superlative," and couldn't stop her legs from squirming.

Indeed, my Johnson flexed in accord.

We're not out of this yet, my subconscious pointed out. *We won't have to worry about the cops for a minute - the entire force is back there - but only for a minute.*

"Right," I murmured. "We can pervert later."

We had to get out of this enormous eye and ear magnet. Vehicles didn't get any more conspicuous than this, huh? We needed a more nondescript ride. Or a good hiding place.

Clutch, shift, *gas.* I raced our behemoth hot rod toward Gulfport, turning too quickly down heavily trafficked roads, at one point going up on two wheels, crushing the sides of an entire row of cars parked at a curb, nearly overturning us. The girls screamed at me, curses coupled with facts about the Bronco's top-heavy disposition. I giggled at their voices, scolding tones vibrating from the mud tires' moan and rumble, mind-numbingly loud exhaust that shook our seats and vision.

I squinted hard to focus up ahead, the only woods for miles in sight. I steered toward the trees with a burbling elation in my throat, tongue hanging out, thinking we had beaten Team Law, when a state trooper blipped in the rearview mirror, passing through the intersection behind us.

Blondie noticed my eyes locked onto the mirror. "What is it, Babe?" She turned to look out the back, pulling a lock of hair over an ear. She pounded the seat. "Fricken crap!"

The trooper didn't slow and endeavor a reasonable turnaround. He showed us he was a worthy opponent, whipping his ride sideways, dust cloud spiraling up, tires blackening the intersection, lights blazing on in mid-turn. His Crown Victoria lurched, racing quickly in our direction.

"He'll have friends!" Shocker said, tone suggesting she had a history with the highway patrol.

"Don't worry!" I said stoically. "They can't follow us through the woods!"

My confidence transmitted to the engine, RPM gauge climbing into the red, eight hundred balanced-and-blueprinted horses galloping combustion that rattled our teeth, extreme full-body massage. *What is the speed rating for those Boggers???* I wondered briefly. Any faster and centrifugal force could throw that heavy tread off the wheels.

Visions of a fiery crash lightened my press on the throttle. Blondie gestured at the trees approaching fast, an undeveloped area of maybe twenty acres. "You know these woods?"

I shrugged, unconcerned. "Woods are woods with a ride like this!"

I felt Shocker's firecracker glare on me. She sighed and got on her phone. Put it on speaker. "You tracking me?" she yelled.

"Yes dear," Ace answered. We could barely hear him. I let off the gas a little more.

"We're going into some woods! What's in them and on the other side?"

I pictured the geek sitting in his car, angular face illuminated by the tablet on his lap. Bobby looking on from the passenger seat. *Anh Long's* hooded eyes and Crystal's pie eyes curious from the back seat. Ace's Galaxy *Note* was not his only source of computing power; the tablet was Entangled with the giant computer at my garage, his Big Black Wrecker- a hacker's wet dream rig, according to Blondie. The geek's equipment gave him scary power. I wouldn't be surprised if he was watching us from live satellite feed. He said, "On the other side is an industrial complex. A large one."

"Can we make it through the woods?" she wanted to know.

I frowned at her, *Please.*

Ace said, "The topographical images of that grid show hills but no visible obstructions. But, uh, they're old."

Shocker's head shook, *Not good enough.* She didn't like the unknown. "Find us a route!"

"Yes, dear."

Downshift, brake. The moan of tires dropped to a low warble, engine winding down. Turned us off the road and through a shallow ditch, torquey first gear engaged, all the wonderful chinks and whines of backlash in the heavy-duty drive-train mixing with squeaks and hisses of the Skyjacker suspension, towering pine trees reflecting the intrusive racket. The off-road knobbies were at home, throwing rooster tails of dirt, pine straw, leaves and sticks on the patrol car attempting to follow us. His siren blared annoyingly.

The plot of woods angled up, steep hill of loose, dead flora providing little traction on the surface, massive truck sinking its tires into the soil below like a prehistoric carnivore clawing its way to freedom from a pursuing tribe of hunters.

A glance behind us showed me our tail was no longer a threat. The Crown Vic' was sunk in our ruts sixty yards back, trooper standing behind his open door with a radio to his lips. He snatched his wide-brim hat off and gesticulated with profanity. Blondie watched him too, hand to her mouth, eyes bright with excitement.

The trees were too thick to see through in some places, though weren't large enough to impede Broncostein. Small saplings, mostly hardwoods little bigger than my arm, went down under the massive bumper, lying flat along our trail, showing the impressive swath we cut through the vegetation. A tangle of Muscadine vines caught in the winch, stretching down from a magnolia my door scrubbed against, breaking, elastic force snagging the mirror right off the door.

We approached the top of the hill, a quarter mile from the road that now crawled with law enforcement. I pushed the gas pedal to its stop, front-end going over the summit, tires leaving the earth, autumn sky then big tree appearing through the windshield.

"Ah!" the girls yelled in chorus, wincing, taking the impact on arms that gripped the dashboard handle.

The tree, a magnolia larger than my waist, didn't possess quite enough mass to refute the Bronco's desire to bulldoze over it. It slowly toppled, bumper grinding up the trunk, shaving off thick slabs of bark, green wood scent mingling with the hydrocarbons of the furious exhaust. Super Swampers digging for more purchase, sliding us over the state tree's branches, roots splitting, giving way in jolts, top of the magnolia crashing on the ground in impressive fashion, taking down several lesser trees with it.

"Yeah!" I cackled in winning spirit as we cleared the obstacle, the three of us leaning forward now that we headed downhill. Weaved around a giant oak, ramping a rotted log, gravity lending us speed.

The girl-beast's eyes glistened with our feat, chest heaving in the black suit, forcing herself to take slow breaths. My girl looked much the same, riding along on all those same baffling chemicals our bodies produce when we're terrified and exultant and horny and ready to fight or run for our lives- in this case, all at the same time.

I had my own brew of hormones and neurotransmitters I was sipping on, drugging me with infinite, frightening euphoria, amplified by my sensitivity to the girls. I was walking the edge, confident I wouldn't slip, not fearing the certain death if I did. The thrilling, in-the-moment feeling... *exquisite.* Which is why the abrupt influx of panic was sooo fuck-you-very-much unwelcome.

Six disbelieving eyes stared out the windshield as I braked to gain perspective of our newest predicament. We were in a valley of sorts, between two large wooded hills. And at the bottom?

A stinking-ass swamp!

"How unfortunate," I said.

"Fuck," Shocker agreed.

It wasn't an old Cyprus-type of swamp, at least. It was a newer one. One with soupy runoff from the red clay hills, with patches of pond scum and broken drainage pipes. One that will probably be the hurdle we can't jump. There was no way around it.

I looked at Blondie. We communicated with a glance, opening our doors and jumping out, pine straw crunching, softening the seven foot drop. Quickly, with experienced hands, we knelt by the front tires and grabbed the slotted mechanisms in the center of the wheels, turning the Warn hubs, feeling the click that signaled the front wheels were engaged and ready to bust some turf.

In a moment of madness, perhaps from the 180° change from arousing confidence to deflated uncertainty, I could swear the Super Swampers were angry with me. The knobbies beetled like pissed off brows, *Now you invite us to the party???* Like a petulant lover they accused, *You're using me!*

"Uh," I said.

"High or low?" Shocker asked as we climbed back in, closed the doors.

"High!" I said, pushing the clutch in.

Shocker grabbed the transfer case shifter between her legs, pulled it back then over to 4-HIGH, a gear selection that engaged all four wheels without sacrificing speed.

As I revved the big block and prepared to test just how Super the Swampers actually were, pistols cracked behind us. Apparently our trail blazing wasn't any faster than a doughnut eater could run through the woods. The bastard had caught up to us, and brought his pals.

"Go!" Blondie yelled, ducking, covering her face. The back window shattered in a spray of glass shards that rained down on our heads.

I needed no urging. I launched us down the hill, racing toward the soggy bottom, frantically searching the terrain for the path of least resistance. And not finding it. "Straight into it, then," I muttered, shifting into second, gaining momentum I hoped would carry us across the wide mud pit.

The speedometer hovered around 40 mph, an insane speed for this terrain, when Broncostein plowed into the business. Huge waves of soupy mud shot out to the sides of the Ford, spraying dozens of feet with great pressure, chunks of clay mixed with light brown water raining on the hood, roof, windshield completely covered, blocking any view. The roaring exhaust suddenly muted, and I knew the fat tail pipes were thrusting hot muck like jetivators under the surface.

Momentum slowed almost instantly, bodies thrown forward. I feared our heroic Ford was overmatched, but the tires kept digging and slinging, hood just under the waterline, 800 hp barge pushing through the Mississippi mud with mechanical determination.

The girls looked at the brown painted windshield with wide-eyed apprehension. Shocker yelled, "Turn the wipers on!"

"They're on!" I yelled back, re-checking the switch, fascinated by the deluge so thick we couldn't even see the wipers at work.

I rolled down my window. Flinching away from the spray the front tire slung back over the door, spatter covering my arm. Stuck my head out for a quick peek, squinting through the liquid dirt that instantly covered my face. Glimpsed the Finish line a hundred feet away.

Blondie found a shirt on the back seat, tossed it to me. I wiped my mug, white-knuckled clench on the wheel, concentrating on the truck's movement through the sludge, sensing we were sinking deeper, slowing. *Not good...* The speedo' said 35 mph, tires spinning powerfully in second gear, though we were moving maybe 2 mph. We could no longer see the hood. Water poured into my window, flooding the cab. I didn't care because we were about to be through it or stuck. Shocker squawked as water hit her butt, lifting up to shimmy in next to Blondie.

I couldn't believe we weren't stuck yet. The deciding factor, I think, was the locking differentials; most 4-wheel drives have gears that only engage one wheel in the front and one in the back simultaneously. Hard-core off-road guys put positive traction lockers in the differentials to make all four wheels spin at once. Broncostein had top-notch axles and gears, passionately maintained by a mud riding maniac.

Old man Tiblier... I owe him one... Even though he sold Blondie a warped cylinder head and claimed she did it. The dick...

We slowed even further, almost stopping, sinking, girls gasping, gripping the seat and dash as I panicked and banged the tranny into first, tried to push the gas pedal through the floorboard. Relief pushed us back in the seats a moment later, front-end elevating. We had made the other side, sloping upwards. Engine redlining, louder when the pipes cleared the mud, Bronco digging violent ruts five feet deep as it crawled out of the swamp. Feminine cries of victory rang in the cab, but I held off on cheering because we still couldn't see out of the damn windshield.

When it was apparent our ride was on stable terrain once more I chanced getting out to wipe the sludge from our view. I braked, found neutral and swung out on the open door. Turned off the wipers. Raked the shirt over the glass. Glanced behind us. About seven cops stood at the edge of the bog a football field away, pointing, arguing on ways to get around it. One spoke into his phone while staring at me.

"Expect company up ahead," I told the girls, closing the door, gripping the wheel. The smooth hard wood vibrated strongly as the 460 idled. I found first gear and drove us into the trees.

"They'll be there soon if they aren't already," Shocker said. Her brown ponytail struck my arm as she turned to my girl. "Ever play a damsel in distress to trick a cop?"

Blondie gave a wicked grin.

"Is that how you did it?" I said.

She nodded, still looking at Blondie. "I acted like someone had robbed me. I had borrowed a hat and jacket to disguise myself from the police chasing me and Ace. I –"

"Wait. Wait wait wait." I barked a laugh. " 'Borrowed'? You can't even say the word 'stolen'." I nudged her with my elbow. "Come on. Say it. '*I stole a hat and jacket*'."

She didn't appreciate my imitation of her voice. When she looked at me a flash went through her eyes. I was reminded of a TV killer's shadow flickering past a lit up window, sensed by a trick of the eye. She growled, "I borrowed it."

I stuck my tongue out at her. She blew out a breath, chuckled then finished her story to Blondie. "Cops were searching everywhere for us when we escaped MDOC transport vans. One got out to help some poor crying lady and got a big surprise." She rubbed her right fist, laughed. "Broke my hand on his German tank head. But I did get his car and we got away."

I had a cartoon grin. Jangling piano key teeth. I recall their prison break from the news. Because of her fame as a boxer and Ace's infamy as a Wikileaks hacker the story was huge. Two unidentified men, who I now know were Bobby and our coach, had assisted them. And by assisted I mean beat the crap out of four cops. In the end half a dozen cops had been assaulted. One hit by a car. Three had crashed their cars. And one had his car jacked by the Shocker.

Hell yeah. I looked at the girl-beast, nearly stopping to hug her.

The thick brush was mostly sticks, small deciduous trees with a few brown and red straggler leaves clinging here and there. They rattled loose as the Ford monster trudged by, deep piping bellow whipping up the carpet of dead pine straw. Ahead the trees thinned and ended suddenly, a concrete and steel business complex becoming visible. I revved Broncostein and launched us straight over the remaining trees in our path, knowing if any cops were in the vicinity they had plenty of warning from the 800 hp K.W. Cook special under the hood. No sense in trying to sneak around.

There were streets outlining the perimeter of the huge industrial area. Two-story concrete buildings with purposes unknown to me were on the immediate other side. I crossed to them quickly, tires coming out of the dirt, gripping the pavement with a bark, pinning us in the seats. Braked, turned, gassing it, hoping to find a spot to stash this behemoth. We had to get it off the road, asap.

"There! Left, Babe!" Blondie pointed.

Turned, shifted. On the side of some kind of gravel processing factory were two rows of dump trucks, a few cement trucks behind them. I chuckled as we idled by the first Mac; Broncostein's hood was higher. Made me feel like a heavyweight contender.

The exhaust loped and crackled off the huge trucks on either side of us. We parked, relatively out of sight. When I shut off the engine we stared at the dashboard for a moment, three gear heads sharing appreciation for the mechanical wonder that got us this far. The after effects of the roaring, emotional rush made me feel like I had been piloting a NASA rocket while slurping a cocaine shake through a fat straw. Our collective sigh was a little cheesy, so I shooed the girls out, climbing out on their side. Jumped down, turned to look one last time.

The mud and vegetation stuck to the chassis and body was, quite simply, marvelous.

"We could take one of these," Blondie indicated a dump truck.

I shook my head. "We'd be trading one giant, visible vehicle for another." I patted a red Mac fender. "And this one won't ramp police cars or go through swamps."

"True." Blondie's lips pursed, turning wicked again, eyes narrowed in scheme. She looked from me to Shocker. "We'll go will your plan, then. I'll trick him, you clip him."

Shocker nodded seriously. I let the girls call the shots on this one, following close behind their leather and Kevlar clad butts, trying hard not to become distracted. They carried their helmets, Shocker's hiking boots and Blondie's borrowed sandals touching the ground as light as ballerina steps, my Rockports not much louder behind them.

The buildings were concrete and blue sheet metal, some small, most very large. Around the office entrances were sidewalks lined with small flower beds, all empty. For whatever reason, the offices in this area were just as barren. Wide drives curved around and between the buildings, parking slots outside of the smaller ones.

The sun reflected off the Ford Fusion and Toyota Avalon we chanced upon. Squatting down and peering around the corner of a steel wall, Shocker stood above me as we watched the drive beyond the cars and whispered, listening for signs of approach with ears that still itched.

"Any minute now a patrol car will pass," Shocker said. "They'll be spread out, so it should be only one car." I nodded, impressed, remaining quiet. She turned and spoke to Blondie. "They need to see you in distress. But let them pass first so you won't be in view of their dashboard camera."

A mocking bird landed on the roof of the Toyota, chirping. As if commenting on the beauty of it I told Shocker, "I believe you are a born criminal."

She sighed, "Shut up."

"I got this," Blondie said, nonchalant. She handed me her helmet.

I watched her long legs and flexing, tight leather cakes as she jogged to the cars, ducked down between them. Sitting on her heels, she peered over the Avalon's door, then the Fusion's, checking both sides of the street through the windows. We didn't have to wait long. The radiator cooling fan of a Crown Victoria Interceptor whirred off the buildings to our right, V8 exhaust notes close behind. It wasn't in a hurry, which meant the driver was taking a careful look around.

Please don't have a friend, I thought.

As the black and white approached the Avalon, Blondie inched around the back of it, keeping the car between her and the cop. Shocker and I ducked out of sight, knowing Blondie would stop him before he got far enough down the street to see us.

Errrt! The cop hit the brakes. We heard the shriek of a wounded woman and his door open. We stuck our heads around to see the show.

"Please!" Blondie wailed at the cop, a tall blonde deputy sheriff that poked his chest out importantly. If Abercrombie made uniforms he'd be their model. "Please help! They took my bike!"

The deputy hurried over to the beautiful motorcycle chick that had magically appeared behind his car. He grabbed her shoulders to steady her shaky balance. "Are you okay? Tell me what happened."

Blondie looked up at him from under hair pulled out in wild puffs, eyes glassy with emotional trauma. The girl could act. She suddenly screamed at him, grabbing his uniform. "You didn't see them?!"

"No. Uh –"

"That's because they're right behind you!"

The man jerked around, going for his gun. His eyes bulged at seeing the girl-beast an arm's length away. Her face was twisted in Destroy mode, all coiled scariness that momentarily stunned the man. I stood behind her holding the helmets, casually bored, the boyfriend tricked into coming along just to carry the shopping bags. "Hey," I told him in a disinterested voice.

Shocker didn't give him the chance to clear his weapon from the holster, lunging in with a straight-right, blistering quick. I thought she was going for the lower abdomen, and clucked my tongue in surprise when I saw her knuckles sink into his wrist. The likely fractured, paralyzed hand dropped the gun in a metal clatter. Her left fist hit him a millisecond later, twisting shoulders and torqueing hips throwing a bombing hook that began in her thrusting left foot and ended after impacting on his open mouth, jaw wrenching sharply, making a sound like a cough suddenly cut off. The girl-beast's battle cry echoed throughout the quiet buildings.

Not wanting to be out-done, Blondie showed off her right-hand, left-hook combo. Before Shocker's blows fully registered on their mark she stepped forward with teeth bared, pushing hard off her back foot, right fist driving into the man's kidney, left-hook digging into his lower ribs a blink later, *boomp-boomp!* Her battle expulsions were loud feminine breaths rather than roars of power, like a tennis champ pounding out a 120 mph serve.

He got served alright, I snickered in thought.

The attack from both sides with such ferocity and precision of strikes was too much for the pretty boy's nervous system. From the time he stepped out to help the "victim" to the time he lay on the pavement took maybe seven seconds. The two gorgeous fighters stood over him with balled fists, slightly open mouths huffing killer instinct, making sure the target was eliminated.

This was a scene I could watch over and over for the rest of my life.

"Stop giggling and get in the car," Shocker told me, taking her helmet back. She walked over and leaned into the driver's side of the patrol car. Came back out holding a black pump-action shotgun. Handed it to me. Blondie grabbed the dropped pistol.

"What's this for?" I said, eyeing the weapon.

Shocker looked at Blondie, jerked her head at me like, *Men, huh?* She told me, "To make you feel less inept while I show you how to drive a getaway car."

The girls tittered as they got in the front seats, shut the doors. I got in back, unable to suppress a sullen look. Lay the 12-gauge on the seat.

I had dragged the cop between the Fusion and Avalon. But he'll either wake up or be found soon. We had to get out of this area before that happens. Blondie and I stayed on the floorboards, Shocker driving us toward the complex exit like a deputy that had finished patrolling the area, in no rush, mild window tint enough to fool other cops of her identity from a distance. Another deputy circled a building far to our left. Shocker waved at them. The silhouette behind the wheel waved back, turned to go around another building, where an absolute swarm of law enforcement was massing for a grid search. I let out a breath, peeking out the back window, head low.

Shocker put her phone on the seat. Ace was on the speaker. "Get to Highway Forty-nine," he said. "I have control of the lights south of the interstate."

Shocker looked back at me. I said, "Perfect. We may use that. We'll ditch this –"

"One-o-nine," the radio on the dashboard said loudly, freezing my mouth. We were in 109.

"Um," Shocker said, biting her lip. "Give us a minute, Ace." She turned out of the industrial area, onto a road that led to the highway, acceleration pushing us into the seats.

"One-o-nine?"

"Give it here!" I leaned over through the open Plexiglas partition, taking the mic, stretching the spiral cord. I pressed the transmit button and mumbled the universal situation-is-secure, realizing that cop must have called in Blondie's distressed presence. "Code four on that last traffic."

We held our breath for several seconds, thinking it worked or at least wasn't so bad of an error that dispatch would follow up. Irritation cut me as the radio said, "Brian? You okay?"

"She probably swoons over the Abercrombie prick," I muttered.

"Huh?" Shocker frowned.

"Nevermind." I looked at my girl.

"I'm on it." She curled up on the floorboard again, hands going under the dash to find the wire harness for the GPS.

* * *

The breeze flowing in the front windows was cool, but the car was hotter than a lucrative crack house. In the eight minutes it took for us to get to Highway 49, several hundred law enforcement officers were put on alert. The GPS was disabled, so they couldn't track our position, and the roads we used up until now were mostly without traffic. Listening to the officers on the radio helped, though they were aware of it and used codes none of us were familiar with. The real boon was Ace. He tracked us by his wife's iPhone, and somehow knew where all the cops were. Even Blondie, a contender in the hacking world, was baffled by the geek's computing mojo.

Could he really have hacked into the police, sheriff, and highway patrol systems all at once? I laughed, "Probably has an app for it." Didn't seem possible, yet he knew, and twice already gave us warning so that Shocker could steer us close to a tall truck for cover. We cruised under the Interstate 10 overpass, Blondie and I still laying low.

"They're all over forty-nine north," Ace said, voice smug on the tiny speaker. "Bobby called in an anonymous tip, claiming he saw people in Lyman that weren't cops ditch a cop car. You guys should be in the clear now."

"Oh, that's what's up," Blondie purred. She looked at Shocker, who still paid close attention to oncoming traffic and the sides of the highway, though had slowed some and relaxed her grip on the wheel. "Bobby's a good friend, huh?"

Shocker smiled wide. "I met him at a casino years ago. He was in a suite across from me." She sighed with thoughts of another lifetime. I tried hard to block out their girl-talk but my damn ears betrayed me. "He was competing in a bodybuilder contest the same night I had a fight there. So of course we had VIP passes to all sorts of event crap. Kept running into each other. Eventually we quit just saying hi and had a conversation. Turned out, he was an auto paint and body specialist, and I just happened to be looking to hire one for my shop. The man knows metal and paint." She beamed with pride.

"Boss," Bobby's baritone strained the phone's speaker, a smile in it. "Don't start telling all my secrets now."

"Yeah," Ace concurred, laughing with his friend. "Don't tell how the man writes code. Like Razor said, I thought women were supposed to talk about men behind their back."

Blondie smirked. "He still calls you 'Boss' though he treats you like a sister."

"He better," Shocker laughed. "We've been through so much. And he's never had a better friend than Ace. Those two…"

Ah. Relief. The 'ol fingers-in-the-ears-while-humming was childish, sure, but effective. I hummed *All Along the Watchtower* by Jimi Hendrix while stretched out on the cramped backseat. As I finished and started flipping through my mental collection of music, my right finger abruptly jammed deep into my ear, car lurching forward, transmission dropping into first as Shocker punched it to run.

"Ouch." Grimacing, I strained to sit up. The g force from the accelerating V8 didn't help. I was tired and hungover from consuming all that adrenaline. One look out the back window perked me right back up, however.

Heart pounding excitedly, eyes alert and sharp once more, I studied the Gulfport police cars right on our ass. Two of 'em. Ace shouted something and the lights of the intersection we approached turned green, multiple cars coming from east and west locking up their brakes. Metal crumpled and screeched as it tore, a bumper flew over our hood. Shocker's expert driving took us through the obstacles, lights turning red as we passed. More brakes squealed as traffic packed closer together. I turned to look out the back again in time to see a full-size pickup towing a boat crash into a police car, crushing the front-end, trailer jack-knifing, boat turning over on top of a Honda Civic. More Gulfport PD turned onto the highway, having found a path around the intersection, five cruisers speeding to catch up to us.

Thrilled, I unzipped my suit, wiggled a hand into my jeans and pulled out my BlackBerry. Turned and recorded the scene. "That's right," I gloated, nodding at the awesome footage. "That's what I'm talking about!"

"What are you doing?" Shocker yelled at me.

I put my phone away. Zipped up. "Relax and drive, woman. It's not like –"

WHAM!

Out of nowhere a car crashed into our right side. The tremendous impact instantly stuck us to the passenger doors, painfully, Shocker on top of Blondie, exploding glass showering our heads, seats, floor and dash. Our car skidded on blown tires, spun halfway around, steel wheels on pavement making all kinds of tortured racket. We spun back straight, still skidding at high speed then crashed into something on our left that threw everyone to that side of the car.

We ground to a halt, engine stalling.

My head rung, body numb in places, and I just wanted to lay there. But a part of me was activating emergency reserves, booting up Escape and Survive functions. Panic, fiery and alien, swelled in my gut. Something was badly wrong, though it wasn't with me. I saw something that wasn't registering yet. My arms and legs twitched. A voice in my head yelled, "Get your ass up NOW!"

I scrambled up to look around. Only seconds had passed. Behind and to our right was the police car that rammed us, huge black tubular bumper deformed, officer unmoving behind his deployed airbag. I looked left. The concrete divider we smashed against had flattened the doors on that side. The glass in all four doors was missing, particles winking from all over, even the girls' hair, which would look dazzling if blood wasn't staining Blondie's disarrayed golden locks...

In a moment of sheer terror I realized both girls were unconscious, Blondie seriously hurt. Her door had taken the full impact of the crash. It was caved in, plastic panels and metal frame bent, stretched over her leg. I had my head through the partition, teeth clenched, head swimming, poisoned by the sight of my girl's slack, bleeding mouth.

Time froze. Thoughts raced. *Is she breathing? She can't be... dead?*

My vision blurred, cheeks cool as wind touched the tears on them. I gulped a breath, struggling with a constricted throat. I shouted furiously. I didn't have time for feelings!

Knowing the doors would be jammed and it would be awkward and time consuming to shimmy out a window, I didn't waste time in that direction. Pressing my back against the partition, I kicked out the back window, boot going right through, glass bits exploding onto the trunk lid. I was up and out of the car, stomping over the roof and, two heart-beats later, kicking in the windshield. It took several hard, bone-jarring heel strikes, caving, spider-webbed glass laying over the airbag. At that point Shocker had roused herself and managed to fight loose of the airbag and help me get the glass out of the car. I tossed it aside, dropped to my knees and reached for my girl.

"Get off the car and lie down on the ground!" some asshole yelled. "We will shoot you!" Boots thumped and noisy weapons belts could be heard distantly.

"She's stuck!" Shocker said, straining, pulling Blondie's arm. "We have to leave her!" She let go and climbed out over the steering wheel.

"NO!" I shouted in a ragged voice, wiping my eyes. "I'm taking her home."

Shocker blew out a frustrated breath. Then dove headfirst back into the car, grabbing the pistol Blondie had dropped on the seat. I helped her back out. We slid off the hood, squatted in front of the car, try-ing not to inhale the antifreeze steaming out of the grill. She held the gun up in front of a face covered with blood, tiny cuts on her cheeks, brows and scalp leaking. She wiped her forehead, wincing as glass was pushed further into her face. With true warrior spirit she pre-tended the blood wasn't leaking faster now. She looked into my eyes. "I'll draw them off. You get her out." I nodded and choked back a sob. She said to herself, "Always the hard way," and suddenly jumped over the concrete divider, into the opposing lanes of traffic, which hadn't been stopped yet. Shouts for her to freeze were ignored. She sprinted away some distance. Stopped in the middle of the highway, turned and aimed over the roofs of passing cars, firing one shot at a police car, then turned and ran again, knowing they couldn't shoot at her because of the heavy traffic. Cars honked and accelerated or braked to avoid the lunatic woman with the gun.

Squealing tires, screams and shouting policemen competed with sirens and racing engines in a dissonance bout, chaos I tried to tune out so I could focus on getting my girl free. Antifreeze caused me to slip on the hood. I grabbed the windshield frame and cut my palm on shards of glass. Didn't feel it. A sob burst from my lips as I crawled in to inspect the door crushed over her. I stroked her cheek. "I got you," I whispered fervently.

Another gunshot sounded, this one from far beyond the cops, and it dawned on me Shocker was circling them, keeping traffic between them.

They'll never catch her on foot, my subconscious reassured me.

I knew the risk she was taking for us and didn't want it to be for nothing. I had no time. I needed a solution.

I looked through the partition, out the busted back window. A squad of officers in tactical gear were forming up next to an armored truck seventy yards away, M-16s in hand. *Never had Special Weapons And Tactics after me before...* They will rush this car and kill us both in just a minute.

I looked at the car that rammed us. It sat in the far right lane, a few dozen feet away. Several uniformed policemen were pointing pistols at me from behind the open doors, their unconscious comrade being carried away by others.

I looked down into the backseat, heart soaring. *The shotgun!* Quickly I reached for it, pulled it through the partition. Jacked a round into the chamber, *shick-click!* Cops yelled for me to drop it. I looked at the wrecked door. At the helmets on the floor. Laying the weapon aside, I grabbed Blondie's helmet and pulled it over her head, carefully, hoping I wasn't damaging anything in her neck. Secured the chin strap. Then I tugged on Shocker's helmet. I pulled Blondie towards me and aimed the shotgun at the door pillar where I knew the latch was. Pulled the trigger.

BOOM!

Flame belched brightly, ears deafened instantly from the concussion. I unloaded the weapon into the door and pillar, pumping the action as fast as I could. Bits of metal, plastic and lead shot ricocheted into her still form, *thwacking* off our helmets, leather and Kevlar preventing penetration. The door was on fire now, smoldering toxic fumes, and a new fear gripped me.

She's going to be burned!

The gun clicked empty and I dropped it on the floor. Raised my right leg over her and began hammering at the door with my heel, over and over, raging with bestial energy. The frantic, inhuman power pulsing through my core was terrifying to experience. In a moment of insane clarity I knew a fear more pure and bodied than I could have imagined. It drove me. It was a revelation. Love or fear alone wouldn't be enough emotional juice to accomplish this Herculean task. But love and fear together, fear of *losing* my love…

Stomp! Stomp! Stomp! I snarled viciously, jackhammering my leg. Suddenly, my boot was in sunlight, door sagging open, off her. Flames shot up as air hit the door panel. Hope soared through me. "I got you," I whispered, grabbing under her arms.

"Get out of the car, now! Get on the ground or we will shoot you!"

I sneered at them.

I climbed out the front and pulled Blondie's limp form over the dashboard, onto the hood. A SWAT officer fired at me, rifle bullet nailing my shoulder pad, knocking me off the car. My head swam, low on energy after the feat of getting her free. I grabbed her, stumbling to cradle her, looking up as a pistol fired.

The SWAT members ducked and were forced to reposition their shields as the Shocker fired at them, her ponytail streaming out behind her black suit as she sprinted away, just outside their perimeter, a ghostly fast streak with a scarlet face.

Seeing that she was the imminent threat, the majority of the officers hurriedly reformed and began methodically moving in her direction, expanding the net. Multiple black and whites peeled out and raced toward the businesses she had disappeared behind. I watched for an apprehensive moment, hoping her crazy ass could shake them. I hefted my girl over one shoulder, arm wrapped around the backs of her knees. Stepped over the concrete divider.

As I got a leg over several pistols fired and bullets struck us. Blondie's helmet resounded with a cracking *pop!,* the supersonic force knocking her head to the side. My sight tinted red, flushing with hot rage. A second round followed, thudding into my lower back, just missing the vertebrae, which surely would have fractured and ended this. Red changed to black, eyes blinking swiftly, core muscles contracting in odd contortions.

"*Gah-rrr!*" I gritted my teeth so hard I thought my molars would burst. Fell to my knees, struggling with a suddenly weakened left leg.

Not like that leg was worth much, anyway, my subconscious offered cheerfully.

"*Gah-rrr!*" I responded, getting back up. Blondie's buck twenty-five now felt twice as heavy. I staggered out into the lanes without awareness, no peripheral in the helmet, and almost saved the police from any further effort. A line of cars braked hard, several swerving at the last instant. I was pretty sure everyone else had stopped or wrecked so I gave a drunken thumbs up to the pissed off, screaming, gesticulating motorists and staggered off to the other side. As I looked at them I wondered how come traffic was still flowing, though was glad for the protection it provided. Then it dawned on me the police hadn't had time to stop it yet, only a few minutes had passed since the wreck. It seemed like hours ago.

I knew cops would be on the other side of the highway momentarily, though not near as many; the brunt of the force was concentrated at the scene or chasing Shocker. I limped as quickly as I could across the emergency lane, into the grassy ditch lining the east side of the highway, helmet swinging left, right, searching for patrol cars. Spotted several speeding our way through traffic in the distant intersection, lights and sirens pushing the other drivers aside.

Limp-limp-limp! I lurched toward a road, gasping in pain, pissed because it was a chore to even focus my eyes. I had to really dig deep here, get some control of my leg. It was starting to loosen up, though this wasn't a minor contusion I could just walk off. That bullet *hurt,* Kevlar be damned. My shoulder pads had taken rounds from a rifle and pistol. My entire upper back was stiff, aching, from SKS rounds that drove the padding between my shoulder blades. And my side took one that likely cracked a rib. But none of those mattered any longer. Nuclear plasma was melting through my lower back, arresting command of the sciatic nerves that somehow still functioned enough to allow me to use the leg as a crutch.

I'm all for a challenge, folks, but this was getting ridiculous.

Only seconds until the patrol cars reached us. I needed to circle some buildings to buy us time. Panic began to well up my throat again. I just didn't have it in me. Usually I'm chuckling like a stoned Goofy in situations like this. But usually my bitch is by my side, stoned-Goofy-chuckling with me. I felt incapable of tapping into that fighting fuel I knew was just outside my exhausted mental reach. I felt like a lame.

Then I heard a sound that changed everything: Blondie moaned. I stumbled, rebalanced, straining my hearing, and one of her dangling arms reached up and grabbed my waist.

She's okay!

Her touch was all I needed. Relief was an energy all its own, overwhelming me. I began to run. I leaned forward and lengthened my stride, trying not to jolt her too much, looking for a ride I could take without too much fuss. I ran behind a tire and wheel shop, cop cruisers turning in behind us, and continued around the building, circling it, running back out front before crossing the street to zig-zag between two fast-food joints. Turned down a narrow lane and spotted a small parking lot in front of a custom car stereo business. Ran to it, optimism expanding my veins at the sight of our ride.

Next to a tricked out Dodge Dart was a Can-Am Spyder, a reverse-trike that looked like a jetski with two wheels in the front, one in the back. Like anyone with a love for custom 'cycles, I've wanted to ride one since they came out. Supposedly, they performed like road course race cars.

"We're about to find out," I told Blondie, taking her off my shoulder. I strained to turn her, straddle her over the seat, lay her over the fuel tank. I squatted down next to the fairing, hands digging under the plastic in search of the ignition wires. Through her face shield I could see her eyes fluttering, our helmets nearly touching. "Babe? You okay?" No response. "Shit."

"Hey! What the hell do you think you're doing?"

My head jerked up, dread enveloping me like a thick nasty fog. A mountain of a man came out of the stereo shop. His pink-white bald head looked small on his wide neck. Eyes small because of flaring cheeks. He walked quickly towards me, slabs of chest and shoulder muscles shifting under an Audiobahn tee shirt, pointing a meaty, threatening finger.

We don't have time for this!

I opened my face shield. "We're from Can-Am. Gotta take it in. Sorry. Call the office if you have any complaints."

"I'm not calling anybody – you're not going to take it!" He walked quicker, scowling. He pointed at Blondie. "Get that bitch of my bike!"

My eyes locked onto his, deep, rumbling growl issuing from my chest. It was a bad choice of words, for many reasons. First of all, *I'm* the only one that gets to call her that, and only in an endearing manner. And furthermore, well, he should be able to see she's hurt and needs help and therefore shouldn't be such a dick smoker about me stealing his Spyder.

Lame rationalization, I know. Fuck you for noticing. He probably thinks she's drunk or drugged and I'm just a thief. But the take home message for this guy is this: a desperate man is a very dangerous man. That's something he'll ponder later, after contemplating how a much smaller guy could knock him out.

I narrowed my eyes, seeing geometric lines trace out from me to him to the ground. The physics of punching is fairly straight forward. Coil to strike, and you have potential energy. Throw it and the punch becomes kinetic energy. Velocity equals distance over time. The longer the limb, the faster a punch can potentially move; more time to increase velocity. The faster a fist moves, the greater its momentum and the bigger the exchange of energy when it hits something.

Out of curiosity, Blondie and I once used a 70 lb. bag outfitted with sensors to test our power and speed against other boxers and non-boxers. The average person with no training can generate about 100 psi of punching force, with a fist speed of 15 mph. Elite fighters averaged 776 psi and 23 mph - deadly knockout power. Blondie can throw an overhand-right with 350 psi of force, her little fist traveling 20 mph. Extremely impressive for a chick.

And my very best punch you ask?

800 psi at 32 mph. That's enough force to accelerate someone's head over 40 g - forty times the force of gravity. Most car accidents, lethal ones, involve smashing forces of 30 g to 60 g.

Old coaches used to describe my punches as "murderous". A lovely word to sum up skill developed from many years training as a boxer with an engineer's education.

A fist in motion carries momentum, resisting change until it collides with, say, someone's face. At that point "impulse" applies – a change in momentum. Kinetic energy is transferred from the moving fist to the receiving jaw. Fist slows down while the jaw – and rest of head – accelerates, absorbing momentum to move in the same direction as the fist.

I felt this guy wouldn't appreciate the physics lesson so I kept it to myself. As soon as he stepped in my face I shifted weight onto my right leg, stepping back slightly with knee bent, left shoulder pointed at him, which will give my right fist more time to build up speed. He opened his mouth to further curse me and I unleashed the coiled, potential energy, twitching fast off my back foot, leg straightening to throw my entire weight in his direction, shoulders twisting simultaneously, arm extending, fist speed increasing, faster, faster, his face right at the end of my range where my punch would reach full velocity...

BWAP!

The kinetic exchange was bolstered by my tightened fist, punch hitting his chin with enough force to put him in a neck brace for a month.

His head whipped straight back as if made from foam, eyes squinting shut, flapping open, rolling white. He stumbled backwards on legs that didn't know his brain was temporarily out of order. Fell on his side in a cartoonish posture, puffing like he had sleep apnea. I skipped over and felt his pockets, dug in the one with keys. Grabbed them and lunged back to the Spyder. "Call *my* girl a bitch..."

Two, three patrol cars raced down the road and passed the stereo shop right as I drove around the side, Blondie in front of me, leaning over her, holding her between my arms. Shifting, turning onto an unknown road, I twisted the throttle and thought, *They didn't see us. Don't know we have a ride yet...* Still though, we'll be lucky to get away.

I found several side streets, then a neighborhood, just trying to put some distance between us and the police cordon.

I have to get Blondie help. Perry will know a doctor. Then, *Shit. I hope Shocker made it...*

Normally, having my girl's body pressed up against mine while I drove a performance machine would give me a grin and a protrusion. I felt no pleasure this time, though. Finding a long road with no traffic, I opened up the Spyder and raced toward Ocean Springs, mind and body beyond exhausted from such a long ride, knowing it was far from over.

X. We're Coming For You

The key to a satisfying life is to do things full of risk. Things the opposite of comfortable. Things just flat out *bad.*

Of course, there are plenty of instances in life where it's easiest to increase your happiness by simply listening to a favorite song or having a one night stand with a stranger. But on occasion, it's worth seeking out an experience that is new, very hard, unpredictable, or even upsetting – which could mean anything from finally discovering the courage to go sky diving to allowing sex toys into play. The happiest people seek both easy joy and spine-twisting challenges, benefiting from the contrast; without pain, there can be no pleasure.

Pain… So many benefits come from it.

If your work – whatever physical or mental activity that may be– doesn't push you to your limits, every day, then you're just another lame mutt prancing along after the big dogs. People who condition themselves to endure physical or mental pain, constantly, grow from the hardship. They learn about themselves. They discover limitations, and how to extend them. And perhaps most importantly, they learn how to motivate themselves.

What I've learned recently is people who endure pain as a team develop a new sense of fortitude in themselves, and in the other members. Self-respect and respect for my crew has increased, and the overall *esprit de corps* has strengthened significantly. Our work isn't the work of losers – soft, lazy, path-of-least-resistance crap. It's hard. It hurts. Our reach exceeds our grasp, and we see difficulties as challenges rather than threats.

I've learned that when one team member sees another in trouble, they do whatever it takes to help. They understand that doing so will cause them pain, but that it is good for them. Fighters recognize pain as just another communication signal, telling them they've reached their limit – right where they're *supposed* to be. If you're operating at the peak of your limits you're doing everything you can to fulfill the #1 Rule of Being a Bad Motherfucker: overcome all obstacles, whoever or whatever they may be. Our crew was hurt, our allies hurt badly, but that just means we should appreciate our accomplishments even more. We have grown. We have learned.

After our ordeal lesser people would have sought a shoulder to cry their drama on, whining about risking their lives, too much too lose, bluh, bluh. Lame Me would have told Blondie, "I'm sorry I treated life as a game. No more! I love you…" Lame Shocker would have quit, citing her kids or emotional stress as the reason. The same thing for Lame Bobby and Lame Ace. But quitting never entered our minds. In fact, yesterday's incident and loss only *strengthened* our resolve to see this thing through. We couldn't stop now.

No way.

"It's a good thing we're not lame," I told them, the new brand of pride pushing my chest out.

"Speak for yourself," Perry said, under bite sticking out gregariously. He put a hand on his lower back. "With this slipped disc I've been lame for years."

We laughed, standing around Blondie's bed in a small room that smelled of antiseptic. The injured golden goddess was in a white silk gown, long hair flowing over her shoulders in shiny waves, the result of a bath a nurse and I had given her. Head and back elevated on the bed, she had a good view of her ruined right leg in its bright green cast, eyes barely open, dull with the trauma she suffered.

The clinic was one of many in the medical plazas that populated Washington Avenue. It was an orthopedic facility, a new, high-tech joint run by an intelligent man named Dr. Gorman. Perry's friend. He grudgingly helped us, after we promised a significant donation to his charity, allowing Perry to handle the paperwork. He fixed up Blondie's leg, then saw to Shocker's face and my various wounds. Dr. Gorman could be a brusque asshole. I really liked him. Of course, the handful of Vicodin's he gave me possibly influenced my feelings, as I seemed to be just floating around liking everything right then.

"Young lady," Dr. Gorman said with impatience, walking into the room with a clipboard, long white coat stuffed with stethoscope and pens, perfectly combed hair graying over expensive eyeglasses. He stopped at the foot of the bed, glared around at us. Looked at his patient. "You're lucky. Only minor contusions on the brain and lungs. The CT scan showed a clean bill of health, otherwise. You need rest." Blondie closed her eyes. He turned his reproving gaze on me. "Normally I don't allow patients to stay overnight. She needs to be in a hospital, for Christ's sake. So if she's going to stay here it's to *rest*. Understand?"

I held my hands up. "Rest, alright Doc, she'll get it."

"Your CT scan showed contusions from head to toe," he accused me. "Frankly, I don't see how you are even standing."

"I'm a little stiff," I said.

He held up the clipboard like a shield and closed his eyes. "I don't want to know how you sustained such injuries. I just want you to get some rest, and real soon. The drugs won't keep you going forever." He opened his eyes, pointed the clipboard at me.

I kept my opinion to myself. He nodded sharply, lips firmly pressed together. Whirled around, long coat flapping up to show dress pants and conservative wing tips, walked away quickly. A moment later we heard his insistent voice harassing the patient in the next room.

Shocker shook with quiet laughter. Her face was covered with gauze and tape, the result of glass-removing surgery that required sixty-eight (!) stitches. Last night during the operation, face numb and voice slurred, she had joked, "Good thing I already have a man. I look like the Bride of Chucky."

"Again", Ace had responded blandly, more than a touch of horror in his eyes as he stared at his wife.

Shocker gave a drugged giggle at his expression. "Don't you worry, love. We've been here before. You thought my red alien face was cute last time."

"I was just saying that. The laser treatments lasted a year," Ace said with sorrow. "Your face was red for a whole *year*."

She giggled loudly until Dr. Gorman shushed her.

The girl-beast brought me out of my reverie, telling Perry, "Charming friend you have."

"He is, huh?" Perry's tone was sonorous, amused. "He means well. That's all you can ask."

Perry looked around at us with concern. We had slept at the clinic, and looked like it. Fortunately I was able to wash my jeans, shirt and drawers here, and Shocker brought a few gowns for Blondie. Ace managed to track down his wife before the cops did, and they went to the garage to retrieve camera footage and get a few items in case the joint was raided. They found Big Guns already there, with trusted members of the Royal Family, carrying bodies. Cong and Tuan were dead, torsos riddled with bullet wounds, and there was no sign of the kids. I assumed Diep's crew had waited until we left the security of the garage before hitting us. The kidnapping of Carl and Tho was evidently an afterthought.

I hate to think what those boys are going through, I gritted my teeth in thought.

Ace looked at me from his place in a corner chair, blue camo pants and black long sleeve shirt a match to his wife's, Galaxy *Note* glowing softly on his lap. He said, "I downloaded the video files from your garage. Uh." He scratched his chin. "The cameras caught everything."

Shocker looked sick. "I don't want to see it."

I glanced at her, waved at him, *Give it here.* I took the tablet and scrolled through the video files, playing each one. Tho and Carl had been sweeping the first level, Cong and Tuan standing guard by the street entrance, when five Vietnamese mercenaries in combat black ran into view, having come through a fire exit, and sprayed Cong and Tuan from behind with full-auto machine pistols. The Royal Family members danced spasmodically as their bodies filled with bullets in three seconds, then collapsed without getting off a shot.

The video had no sound, but I could still hear the boys' screams as they witnessed the murders. They still held their brooms, swinging them wildly, crying hysterically as they were grabbed and savagely struck by three of the men, Cong's and Tuan's bodies dragged behind cars by the other killers. I became aware of the tablet shaking as an SUV pulled into view and picked up the five mercs and two boys, hands clutching the plastic casing hard enough to make it creak as they sped away.

They came to my place and...

I knew what must have happened. But actually seeing it brought it home.

"Let me take that," Ace said, gently prying his device loose from my claws.

I let go, let out a held-in breath, and tightened my fists, vibrating with malice. I looked at Shocker and said with quiet intensity, "I see why you didn't want to see it."

She looked at her lap, head shaking slowly. She sniffled. "Another kidnapping," she whispered sadly. "Another one."

"Uh," Ace said. "I found a clear shot of the license plate. I can probably track this car by traffic cameras and satellite, see where they went."

"Do it. We'll be leaving for N.O. as soon as it's dark," I said. I cleared my mind, taking a moment to methodically purge my body of the harsh feelings.

They'll come in handy later, but not here.

I turned my attention to Blondie. I stood at the bed rail with her hand between mine. "Babe." Her eyes opened slowly. Bruises marked her forehead and cheek, dark splotches on skin scabbed from glass cuts, bottom lip swollen and glossy with ointment. She was heavily drugged, with a concussion and broken femur and tibia, clean breaks that will heal 100% according to Dr. Gorman. Her bloodshot eyes struggled to focus on me. I told her, "You wanted to see *Anh Long*. He'll be here soon. He's bringing Loc."

"Big Guns?" she whispered.

I shook my head. "He's busy with the Royal Family. He has to make arrangements for Cong and Tuan. They had wives and kids. And he's trying to figure out what happened to the rest of the security team that was supposed to be guarding the Elder Dragon. They vanished."

"Paid off, you think?" Shocker ventured, saying what we all suspected.

"Sure seems like it," Bobby said ominously. The ebony giant stared ahead with hard eyes, sitting on a stool next to Blondie's other bed rail. He frowned at her IV drip and heart monitor.

Blondie croaked with effort, "Diep probably offered them fuckers a better deal. They didn't have roots here like Cong and Tuan. Diep knew who would flip and who wouldn't."

"The offer of money over death can be appealing," Perry said.

I sighed disappointment. "True. But I never thought Gat would flip like that."

"There's no honor anymore. No telling how long that punk was playing us," Bobby said with a menace that filled the room. "Phong and his boys knew just where to hit us." He indicated Blondie. "Even we survivors lost a lot. She'll never be able to go to the boutique again. Her businesses are forfeit. And we may have left the scene in helmets, but there's a good chance some ambitious detective or fed will find a video of us walking into the boutique."

I said, "The boutiques weren't in her name. Investigators may find our faces but they don't know who we are." Shocker cleared her throat. I looked at her and grinned. "Well, they'll know who *you* are. But it's not like you're listed." I gripped Blondie's hand and told my crew, "We have money. We can start over. Tho and Carl can't. We have to get them back."

"Damn right," Bobby said.

Blondie looked at him gratefully. Her eyes turned back to me. She squeezed my fingers in a weak grip. The absence of strength infuriated me. *Look what happened to my woman! Those MFers will PAY...*

She whispered, "I was going to bring them ice cream..." Instead of tears, her face scrunched with anger.

"Why don't we put this conversation on hold until *Anh Long* gets here," Shocker suggested. "He'll know more, and we can plan without speculation."

"While we're waiting for the head honcho and his weird son, I'll tell you a story," Perry said with infectious cheer. We couldn't help but smile at him. He grinned at his mood-enhancing talent and launched into one of his many humorous nursing tales. "I used to work with an R.N. named Troie. She was about ten years younger than me, but was sharper than guys with twice my experience. She was a supervisor on the second floor," he said, referring to the Ocean Springs Hospital. "We went to lunch together sometimes. Troie was a riot, always able to make light of bad situations. You pretty much had to, working around disease and death all the time, or it would get to you." His eyes twinkled. "We took pills for that, too."

"What kind?" I queried, suddenly wanting more.

He smirked at me. "The kind that get you high. Those kind." He boomed a laugh at my What The Hell Dude? expression. "Troie could take any kind of drug and still function at a high level. I couldn't. Where she would become a witty ball of energy, I became a witless pile of sand." He folded his arms and leaned against the wall. "One morning we went to the bank together. We had just worked a double shift and were stoned on Percocet." He closed his eyes, shaking his head and smiling at the memory. "We were in line with several people, and the other tellers had long lines, too. People everywhere. I was behind Troie. She got to the counter, saw the courtesy pen was missing from its chain, and dug in her scrubs pocket for one – we always carried pens. She fished one out, eyes a little glazed behind her glasses, and tried to write with it. It wouldn't work. She shook it out and tried again. The bank teller was apologizing for the missing pen. Troie said,

'I have one' and tried the pen again. In her haste she hadn't looked at the pen closely. She pulled her glasses down and squinted at it, and we all saw it was a rectal thermometer!" Another booming laugh. "Troie didn't miss a beat. She said, 'Damn. Some asshole has my pen'."

We cracked up, small room amplifying our laughter out into the clinic's hall and lobby. We needed a laugh, so this one carried on longer than it should have. Still chuckling, Perry caught his breath and said, "Half the bank was laughing. The tellers were laughing. Troie just gave a wicked smile and told me, "'I'll keep them going, you grab the cash out of the drawers.'" He wheezed into silence, wide shoulders and big belly shaking with mirth.

"Maybe we should recruit Troie," I suggested, only half joking.

"You have enough drugs and jokes," Shocker told me, hands pressed to her cheeks, trying to keep her face from stretching the stitches. With a painful rictus of a smile she turned to Perry. "Stop making me laugh! My face hurts."

"*My face hurts,*" a woman said with a semblance of Shocker's whine, stepping into the crowded room.

We turned to see a tall, brawny figure with blonde curls, a strong jaw and big nose. Large waist pushing tightly on jeans, even larger bosom pushing on a shirt that declared I'M THAT BITC#. She had a carefree presence, one hand in a pocket, the other holding the hand of a little girl in a skirt that would become a prettier, petite version of her mother. The blonde giant looked closer at Shocker and jerked backwards as she realized the extent of the girl-beast's injuries. "Damn, Shock. You really did get fu –" she glanced down at the little girl, "freaked up."

Shocker responded by gripping her face, groan-chuckling.

They moved further into the room and a twelve year old version of Ace appeared behind them. He held his sister Caroline on his hip, eyes widening in alarm at the sight of Shocker. He handed the baby to her. "Hey mom. You okay?" She waved him off, *Nothing new.* He moved long brown hair out of eyes that were straight out of the geek's Y genes, crystal blue. Freckles stretched into a grin at his mom's non-chalance.

"Hey precious." Shocker hefted the baby, kissed her. Caroline blinked and giggled. Shocker then hugged little Ace with her free arm, burying her chin in his hair, sucking in a breath and squeezing her eyes shut, sniffling, obviously suppressing terrible feelings.

Memories, my subconscious provided. *That boy had been kidnapped by the same crooked cops that put her and Ace in prison.*

Ace stood and hugged the boy, put an arm around his wife and daughter. I watched the family curiously. *So that's what it's like...* Nolan didn't have any of the girl-beast's features, and I surmised he was her stepson; when he was born, she was at the beginning of her pro boxing career. The family broke their huddle and an interesting thing occurred to me: I actually cared to wonder about them.

"Hmm," I frowned.

Bobby stood with a wide grin, bumped fists with Nolan, tickled Caroline's cheek. He said to the boy, "How's school in Juarez?" He kept looking at Nolan, but gripped Shocker's shoulder as she turned away from everyone to wipe her eyes.

"Es muy difícil", It's very hard, he replied with a quick flip of his hair, watching his mom.

"Yeah, yeah. School is hard. Been away too long. Nice to see ya," the blonde giant said. She smirked at Shocker, familiar as old friends are. "We're here. Now what's the fuss?" She waited on Shocker to regain composure, looking around at us strangers. Eyes pausing and wagging at Bobby, who apparently had the pleasure of her acquaintance already.

"Hello Patty," Big Swoll said uneasily.

Patty turned and stared me up and down, full of judgment. She looked at Shocker, inclined her head at me. "This the douche you told me about?"

"Mommy!" the little girl said in a scandalized high pitch, frowning severely at Patty.

Patty looked at her daughter. "What? That doesn't count as a curse word. Crap, girl. Find a lollipop or something. Chill."

The room was full of humor, some of it at my expense. I ignored it, looked at Shocker and crossed my arms. "Douche?"

"Yeah. You're kind of a D-bag at times," she said bluntly. "Hi Jasmine." She promptly ignored me, hugging the little girl, whose lips moved silently with the new term, *D-bag?*

"He *is* a douche," Blondie croaked, corner of her puffy mouth turned up.

Patty grinned with horse teeth, shoved me aside and held her hand out to my girl. "Patty."

"Blondie." They squeezed fingertips.

I scowled at the women. "Hi. My name is Outta Here."

"I believe I'll join you," Perry said pushing off the wall, following me into the hallway.

Bobby towered over the women, huge, hulking, though his body language expressed the timidity of a puppy afraid to cross a street full of scary, insanely driven cars. The women fussed and stroked the kids, already talking about matters that didn't concern men. Bobby gave Nolan a look from experience, *You better come with us.*

Nolan watched his mom with uncertainty. The Shocker did a full inspection of her son while questioning his eating habits and recent activities, pausing only long enough to hug him several times, thoroughly embarrassing the poor dude. She declared him healthy and okayed his leave to go with us, then turned her full attention back to Caroline, bouncing her on a hip, speaking softly in a you're-so-precious voice, while Jasmine alternately yammered questions to her about the baby and Blondie's injuries. Nolan's eyes widened comically. He gave Big Swoll a serious nod, *I'm definitely coming.* Bobby put a hand on his shoulder and steered him around Patty, using the boy as a shield. He snapped powerful fingers in front of Ace, *Let's go, geek!*

Ace finished whatever he was doing on the tablet, quickly put it in a cargo pocket. Looked at Shocker with permission-seeking eyes. "Dear?"

"Go," she told him without taking her eyes off Caroline.

I stood in the hall, looking through the doorway at Blondie. She was under attack, unable to answer Jasmine quickly enough before the little dynamo of interrogatories turned back to Shocker and the baby. Patty rattled on to Blondie about some man in her past that had broken her leg. My freaked out stare matched Perry's, Bobby's and Nolan's. Ace just looked confused. "Come on," I said, heading down the hall, passing several rooms with patients. I opened the back exit and inhaled the quiet, fresh air of the parking lot with relief.

"Whew," Perry said theatrically, wiping his forehead.

Ace came out last and shut the door. "What just happened?" he said.

"The room was too small for everyone so we had to leave," Nolan explained to his father.

"Yeah," I said. "That's what happened."

"Beautiful day," Bobby observed, hands on waist, looking toward the trees a few hundred yards away, afternoon sun hovering over them.

"It is," I agreed. I stripped off my shirt, leaned over and started rolling up my jeans, stopping between calves and knees. There were no people in view – this was the employee parking area – and I planned to get a workout while I could. I straightened, looked at Ace. "You bring the leftovers from the garage?"

He nodded. "Steak, salad, some burgers and deviled eggs. Bread."

"I saw a microwave in the nurses' lounge. I'll fix us something," Perry volunteered. Ace handed him the keys to the Scion.

"Perfect. Anyone care to join me?" I gestured at the large paved area, empty lots flanking it. It was in development. Other medical facilities would soon be built. "Plenty of room to run."

"Why not?" Bobby rumbled, taking his shirt off.

Ace shrugged and emptied his pockets, piling everything on top of the long sleeve shirt he doffed and dropped on the sidewalk.

Nolan looked at us curiously for a moment. *You guys are exercising here???* Then he sighed and rolled up his baggy skateboarder pants, showing us his skinny, Mexican-sunned torso, piling his shirt on his dad's.

I took off at a brisk pace. They shuffled into a line behind me.

I guesstimated circling the lot was about ten laps to a mile, planning on stopping at that point. By lap four I was far ahead, with Ace and Bobby out-pacing Nolan by a wide margin. Three minutes later I had lapped everyone twice and was sprinting the final lap, stopping where we started, near the clinic's back door. Before the others caught up I was shadowboxing. Jabbing, feigning, weaving my head and stepping around behind a row of nurses' sedans and Dr. Gorman's H2 Hummer.

The air was perfect, thick with end-of-year crispness, faint traces of the distant trees and heavy Washington Avenue traffic. Perspiration began to flow in volume as I picked up the pace, increasing speed of punches and frequency of combinations, punching at a rate that kept a constant burn on my shoulders, stepping explosively, pivoting, lunging to keep persistent strain on my legs, balls of feet heating with friction.

Intensely focused on breathing and relaxing muscles, I had a limited sense of what others were doing. I noticed Bobby's massively wide back flexing parallel to the ground, arms pumping out pushups. Ace and Nolan, athletic but not athletes, caught their breath from the run before dropping down to join Big Swoll's chest and triceps exercise.

Another fifteen minutes had me soaked, lungs like a bellows, forcing me to gasp air quickly. I felt my face was red with exertion, focus slipping as my head heated up, salty sweat running down it, onto my lips. My injured calf was tight, though had performed just fine without the aid of the EAP compression legging. I quit after one last explosive one-two, grunted relief, and walked over to the sidewalk and sat on a bench between the sedans and several dark green rhododendrons. Flower beds were withering behind the shrubs, brown stems reflected brightly by the clean clinic windows. I stretched my arms out on the wooden backrest and checked out Bobby's one-arm pushups. Ace was showing his son the proper form for squats, head up, butt pushed out. They finished a couple more sets and joined me on the bench.

"Didn't think you'd be able to run like that on Vicodin," Bobby told me. He leaned forward, elbows on knees, looking at his sweat drip down and stain the sidewalk.

I gave a thumbs up. "No problem. When I was competing I could run like that after two days of drinking and doing coke-"

Ace elbowed me, *Kid present!*

"Drinking Coca-Cola," I said lamely.

"Yeah. All that sugar is bad for performance," Bobby said just as lamely, looking at Ace with an apology.

Nolan looked at us, offended. "I know what coke is."

"You do?" Ace said, genuinely surprised. His mouth twisted. He seemed to be having an epiphany, and not his pleasant one.

"Dad." Nolan was exasperated. "I live in *Juarez.*"

"But you go to private school."

"Yeah, with La Familia's kids."

"Oh." Ace pondered that, eyes shifting, computing.

Nolan grinned at him, then looked at me. "My mom can run and shadowbox like that."

"No kidding?" I replied.

"She was a world champion."

I smiled a little. "Heard that somewhere."

"Think you can beat her?" He turned on the bench, staring at me.

I gave an amused snort. "Kid, your mom isn't human."

"Neither are you," the Shocker said walking out of the clinic. Jasmine followed, holding Caroline's hand, the baby walking as if she were much older. Patty swaggered out behind them. Her eyes locked onto Bobby's shirtless physique with a predatory gleam, mouth curling with devious intent.

Big Swoll stood and grabbed his shirt, turned his back to us and put it on. "I'll check on the food," he said to no one in particular, walking into the clinic. "Hey Perry!"

I stood and faced Shocker, put my shirt on. "Sometimes being human isn't enough. To beat monsters, you have to become one."

She nodded seriously. "I agree. It's all the collateral damage that bothers me."

"*Mommy,*" Jasmine whispered sternly.

Patty's eyes turned from the direction her crush went and looked at the girl. She flapped a hand in consternation. "Alright!" Then she looked at me and muttered without much sincerity, "Sorry for calling you a douche."

"Sure you are." I smiled at Jasmine. The girl turned to me with a pleased smile. I walked over, wiped a sweaty hand on my shirt and held it out to her. "How do you do, young lady? My name is Razor."

"How do *you* do? My name is Jasmine." Her hand was as wide as three of my fingers, her voice a child's, but she met my eyes and shook my hand like a little CEO. Then she looked at her hand and wrinkled her nose.

Caroline had been watching us, mouth open in wonder. She suddenly giggled at Jasmine and asked her, "You make a stinky?"

Jasmine chortled in a squeaky high tone. The rest of us chuckled at their exchange.

"Smart kid," I told Patty.

She looked at her daughter and tried not to smile. "I guess…"

The girl folded her arms primly and arched an eyebrow, *Excuse me? You know darn well I'm smart!*

"What are you doing?" Ace asked his girl as she pulled off the long sleeves, shoulders rippling in the tank top underneath. She balled up the shirt and through it in his face.

"Going for a run," she answered him. "Watch Caroline."

"Yes dear."

She looked at Patty and Jasmine. "You want to show these boys how it's done?"

"Yeah!" Jasmine squealed. She pumped her tiny arms and started an exaggerated jog in place, sandals tapping, looking at Nolan with her chin lifted, *Girls are better than boys.*

Nolan stuck out his tongue, making a farting sound while showing her a thumbs down.

"Hey, I'm for any excuse to take my clothes off in front of men," Patty said. She pulled off her tee, lay it on the back of the bench. She didn't have a tank underneath, and her smile said we were fortunate she was wearing a bra, a large sturdy thing that strained over massive boobies. Her pale skin glowed, muffin top unembarrassedly hanging over her jeans waist. "Let's show 'em, Shock!" she shouted, then stepped forward throwing heavy jabs that made things flop and jiggle.

Jasmine's sense of etiquette was highly offended as she watched her mother, though she kept any rebuke herself. Her mommy was demonstrating supreme confidence in her own skin, and the strength of the display was more than enough to awe jasmine's disagreements into silence.

The slogan on that shirt, I'M THAT BITC#, was written just for Patty, I decided.

Shocker's eyes glittered with amusement. She had missed Patty as much as the kids. They shared a familiarity that only comes from bonding during hard times. These girls had waded through a lake of fire together. *But where?* I frowned.

Prison cell mates, my subconscious bet. *Shocker was locked up for a couple years. She was part of a convict fight ring that broadcast on the Internet. Bet you Patty was in the fight ring, too.*

"Hmm," I considered. She'll make a nice addition to the crew.

"How many you guys run?" Shocker wanted to know. She put a hand on her hip, all attitude. "One?"

"*Ten,*" I scowled.

"Pfff. We'll do that running backwards." She pumped a fist at me.

"I'm leaving my shirt on," Jasmine told Patty with a prim flip of her long blonde ponytail.

Patty adjusted her bra straps, looked down. "Don't worry about it. Mommy's a big girl, with big clothes that slow her down. This thing is like a parachute." She grabbed her shirt and held it open, then pointed at Jasmine. "You're narrow behind will slice through the air like a kite string." She indicated her considerable rear end. "Mommy's butt is an air brake."

Jasmine pressed a hand to her mouth, her laugh like a tickled song bird.

"Ready?" Shocker asked the girls. Patty flipped curly locks off her shoulders and nodded. Jasmine giggled and started running in place again. Mother and daughter burst into a laughing run, trailing the boxing legend that shot off at a speed I was sure would catch her shoes on fire.

"Hey. Did I miss something?" Perry said in utter amazement, walking out of the clinic with food rolled in paper towels. He stopped and watched the girls run, eyebrows climbing above his sunglasses at the sight of Patty's shirtless form.

Bobby followed him, holding several bottles of vending machine milk and orange juice. His mouth widened with distaste and uncertainty when Patty's jiggling bod came flying around the curve of the lot. She flipped her hair and gave a huge wink for his benefit, passing in front of us. He stared after her, mouth literally hanging open, forgetting he held drinks until Nolan relieved him of the bottles.

"I think she likes you," Nolan observed as if he and Bobby were classmates. He laughed and walked away when Big Swoll shook a playful fist at him, *Don't go there.*

Perry handed out hunks of French bread that had been hollowed out and stuffed with steak and salad, some eggs. The grease soaked paper towel was almost too hot to hold. I sniffed it, stomach excited, and took a bite that was far too large, microwaved meat scalding my tongue, eyes watering. I chewed while sucking in cooling air, the sublime taste overriding any aversion to a seared throat.

Nolan handed me an open bottle of milk, cold, wet. I turned it up. Groaned with pleasure. I could actually feel my muscles respond to the perfect balance of protein, carbs and electrolytes. There's nothing better than cold milk after a workout.

Shocker flew by on her third lap, relaxed arms pushing elbows back, diaphragm expanded. Her form was that of an elite runner, breathing in perfect sync with her legs, inhaling for three steps, exhaling for two, stretching out a long stride, Nikes touching so smoothly only an occasional scrape of loose gravel could be heard.

Wonder what those cops were thinking when they saw that beast of a girl running, I thought. If she hadn't gone into boxing, she could have dominated the world of running. Easily.

Shocker lapped Patty, who maintained a lope impressive for her disposition, then high-fived Jasmine's upheld hand, blasting by the little girl who decided to finish her final laps walking. Shocker finished laps nine and ten in a furious burst of speed, arms and neck deforming with fast-twitch muscle, legs blurring blue camo. The former pound-for-pound champ passed the sedans in front of us and let off the gas. "Whew!" she breathed loudly, head high, taking slow deep breaths. Hands on hips, walking a cool-down lap.

I finished off the steak sub and milk, feeling both inadequate and special to have been schooled by the legend. I didn't have to time our runs to know she had blown me out of the water.

Patty ran one more then quit, walking over to stand on the sidewalk next to me. "Well?" she asked, gasping breaths making her chest expand like a bouncy castle. She grabbed her shirt and wiped her face with it.

"Well what?" I said.

"Could you beat her?"

I glanced at Nolan. Back to her. "You feel threatened by anyone that can beat her?" I countered.

She laughed like that was the funniest thing ever. "Oh god no," she finally got out. She pointed at the walking girl-beast. "No one's ever beaten her."

"So you just wanted to rub that in, huh?"

"You're smart." She grinned at me. "Like an i-douche."

"Thanks. I studied nights and weekends to earn that 'i'."

"Mommy!" Jasmine fumed. She stood by Nolan, glaring at Patty. She crossed her arms. The little shrew stomped her foot and demanded, "Don't be *rude.*"

"Sorry," Patty replied, suppressing a grin. "Am I grounded?"

"Put some clothes on!" Jasmine's exasperated tone was hilarious. Apparently this wasn't the first violation of the dress code.

Shaking my head, I turned away from their fussing. Perry, Bobby and Nolan sat on the bench eating. I tossed my paper towel in a trash can by the clinic's door. Stepped over to Shocker, who was already fully recovered, breathing as calmly as if she were sleeping. She watched Ace attempt to feed Caroline a deviled egg, laughing when their daughter spit it out and declared it "grossy". She looked at me, said, "I shadowboxed earlier," she threw a fast combination, "or otherwise I'd show you how that's done, too."

"No need," I replied with mock sourness. "You've proven your skill enough at the gym. No need to shame me in the parking lot, too."

She raised a brow, *You sure?* then laughed.

I wanted to ask her a gazillion questions, mostly about her pro experience with our coach, bur had to put the inquiry on hold when a black Lincoln MKS rolled around the clinic and parked next to Ace's Scion. The tinted windows prevented seeing the passengers, but I knew who it was and so didn't enact any security precautions.

The Elder Dragon stepped out of the car and glanced around. He met my eyes and I nodded, *We're safe.* Closing the door, he smoothed dark hair above his ears. His eyes looked slightly sunken in, mouth pressed into a thin line. He wore a collar-less button-up, black with large white buttons. When his son stepped out of the passenger side wearing similar attire it clicked that they were dressed for mourning.

I narrowed my eyes in thought. *People are dead because of what we are doing. Too many of our team, not enough of theirs. Kids were taken...* What does that say about me, the so-called leader of the operation?

"Says you need to do a better job," I growled.

The men in black approached silently. I couldn't take my eyes off Loc. He had a trained fighter's grace, weight on the balls of his feet, confident, with no nervous fidgeting of hair or clothes. He must favor his mother because he didn't look anything like *Anh Long* in the face. His chiseled clean shaven jaw and buzz cut head really set him apart. But he did have his father's shoulders, wide for a Viet, and strong, long fingers. He wasn't a natural athlete, though only someone with an experienced eye could tell it. Loc was an ectomorph that had outworked everybody in his Army unit to become a mesomorph. He had to be incredibly dedicated to training, having transformed his body type from Thin Rice Cake to Buff Protein Bar, a considerable genetic feat. Eyes downcast, he couldn't see my esteem for him rise. He stopped two steps behind his father, mindful of his position, calmly focused.

"How's everyone holding up?" I asked *Anh Long,* still watching Loc.

The Elder Dragon grimaced. "Our community comes together in times like these. It's not the first time, and certainly won't be the last. Cong and Tuan had family, wives and children, who we will care for. In time, the women will be encouraged to marry again." He raised his chin. "Our people will persevere."

"Good to know." I noticed everyone was listening, furtively glancing at Loc, the mysterious sniper we've yet to see this close up. I said, "You guys wanted to see Blondie?"

Anh Long looked at Loc. "We do, yes." He looked at me. "*Con Xoan* has something he wishes to convey to you as well."

"You fellas hungry?" Perry said in greeting, smiling broadly. He walked over to shake hands. *Anh Long* gripped his hand with a warm politician's smile. But when Perry tried to shake Loc's hand *Anh Long* quickly grabbed his arm and pushed it away. Perry frowned confusion.

Anh Long gave another disarming smile. "Thank you for the offer, but we have eaten already." He gestured to me. "We are pressed for time." He nodded hello to everyone, grinning brightly at the kids.

I turned toward the clinic door. "Let's see if she's awake."

Our train of nine mobbed down the hallway and piled up in Blondie's room. An offended nurse notified Dr. Gorman, who stormed out of his office and demanded that we let his patient rest. Perry maneuvered out the door to placate him. I leaned over my girl and stroked her forehead, skin smooth, soft and cool.

Her eyes opened slowly, dull with a fresh dose of opiates. She blinked. "Hmmm???"

"Babe. *Anh Long* and Loc are here. They came to sign your cast." I ran a finger over the fiberglass encasing her leg, stopping where it ended mid-thigh, restraining the digit from cruising up the path to the Golden Valley.

Her eyes opened wider, wanting to roll or glare a warning. The effort made her wince, head aching, and I instantly felt sorry. She noticed my contrite expression and quirked a brow slowly, *You look sorry, but why is your hand still there?*

I moved it, shifting over to gently rub her temples.

Anh Long stood at the foot of the bed. He gave Blondie a serious bow, eyes locked onto hers. "On behalf of our community, I wish you a speedy recovery."

"Thanks…" she whispered.

He stepped back and Loc stepped forward, also bowing, though without words. His eyes were closed, brows furrowed as if concentrating or praying passionately, left hand gripping his right fist.

I recognized the gesture: a salute of respect given to another fighter. The military had trained Loc extensively in hand-to-hand. In the same way that I relate everything to boxing, his disciplines were rooted in martial arts.

Loc remained silent, communicating plainly without the need for words. His intensity and posture made it clear he was sorry for not being there for Blondie. He was ashamed, and in apparent agony about his failure to hold his post. A sense of bafflement overcame the non-Asians in the room. This was not something any of us have seen before. The old school formality was alien, though appreciated. It was an epic experience that allowed us to connect to this enigmatic warrior.

"It's okay," Blondie said softly, eyes sad. She wanted to hug him.

His eyes shot open. The smoldering determination in them said, *It is NOT okay. And I will avenge our loss and hurt.*

Loc gave her a sharp nod and shifted to face me. The execution of his gripped-fist salute conveyed no apologies, only a bolstered will to make things right. I returned the salute and bow, keeping my eyes on his. He inhaled with relief. And abruptly spun around and faced his father. He bowed low, head almost waist level, and held that position for a long moment. Everyone forgot to breathe. It was silent but for the beep and click of medical machines and hum of the air conditioner, nurses chatting quietly in the lobby. The bodies in the cramped room seemed to press closer.

Anh Long's voice was very low, but we could hear his every nuance clearly. He made Loc stand up straight, looked him in the face and spoke to us, "*Con Xoan* was unable to help at the boutique because he was tracking Diep's men to the garage. There were seven of them, all ex-military. Two were running counter surveillance." His tone lowered to a deadly serious note. "Loc took them out. Five made it to the garage." The old man looked at each of us in turn. "Diep sent his elite to the garage, what he marked as the primary target. Phong's group was a contingency, positioned at the boutique in case they missed us at the garage." He looked at me and inclined his head at the baby. "If their timing would have been accurate, it would have been much worse."

Breaths were sucked in amid angry murmurs, hearts quickening. There was an instant, unpleasant change in everyone. Loc sensed the shift and dropped his head. Gently, he took his father's hands from his shoulders and left without a glance at anyone. His cat-like steps floated him down the hall silently, his departing aura strongly felt, akin to a pressure being released from the room.

Anh Long sighed heavily and said, "While he was setting a trap for the first two targets the others were speeding to the garage. By the time he cleaned up his mess it was too late to catch up. He had hoped depleting their numbers would be enough. Unfortunately the men were too well-trained for Tuan and Cong."

"It was a damn good effort," Bobby rumbled. "And we appreciate Loc being on the team."

Everyone was nodding, minds busy with the information.

Military trained kill squad? What the fuck have I gotten into???

Anh Long looked pensive. He said, "*Con Xoan* is more emotionally involved in this than he should be. Did you know he lost his family before joining the military?"

Shocker looked at him, voice laced with sympathy. "Yeah. Loc and his fiancée were jumped by the Two-eleven. She was pregnant. The baby died."

Anh Long nodded with strained eyes. "She left him. That baby would have been my grandson." He took a calming breath. "*Con Xoan* is driven by revenge. Hatred is blinding, so I made him a follower in this operation." He narrowed his eyes at me. "Otherwise he would act rashly, eliminating the enemy without prejudice."

"What's wrong with that?" I said. "Let's turn him loose. The more he takes out, the less we'll have to deal with." Shocker frowned at him, though Bobby nodded and flexed in accord.

The Elder Dragon was shaking his head. "When you drag a net, you catch far more than shrimp. Our devices must give the other creatures a chance to escape or we'll destroy the entire habitat."

I understood. "So you think the Tiger Society as a whole is redeemable."

"Absolutely." No hesitation, only complete belief.

I looked around at my crew. They were chewing that over in a positive way. My eyes met *Anh Long's*. "Okay. Let's say we knock the administrators off the totem pole. Who will take their place? You? Your people?"

He gave a secretive smile. "The time and circumstances will decide that."

Faces twisted in irritation. No one liked his damn cryptic responses. I just shrugged and said, "To use your fishing analogies, when we take over their ship, we only get rid of the captain and his personal stooges because we need the rest of the crew to run the ship."

He nodded sagely. "Tiger Society is a big ship."

"Was it Phong?" Blondie whispered hoarsely.

Anh Long shot her a surprised look. Then looked around the floor while considering how to answer. His shoulders sagged. He said, "Yes. Phong was the main instigator that night at the church. He is the reason Loc lost his family."

"But…" Shocker trailed off, confused. "Loc's had plenty of chances to get him." Caroline held her hands up to her mommy, face whiney. Shocker sighed and picked her up, groaning.

"Circumstances," the Elder Dragon said. "It was a hard decision."

"But easy to explain." I rolled a finger, *Let's hear it. No more secrets.* I looked at Nolan and Jasmine. Normally they were talking or doing something without concern for our adult conversation. But after seeing Loc they sat riveted, watching whoever spoke with burning curiosity.

Anh Long grimaced at me with eyes that have overseen many life or death situations. This dude has been calling shots for decades. He's the head of the Dragon Family, a nation-wide organization of criminal and legit interests. He leads an enormous community in San Francisco, where the DF is headquartered, and part of the year helps oversee his home community in Biloxi. He fronted an empire, with responsibilities I couldn't even fathom. The full weight of it all was in his dark eyes as he said, "Men like Phong are important to organizations like ours, yet they rarely get a second chance for their transgressions. I seek to change that. As I've mentioned before, I try to ascertain what influences behavior. I understand the social pressures that led to Phong attacking Loc and his fiancée. So I gave him a choice." He held up a finger. "Live, and work for atonement." Another finger. "Or die. He chose wisely."

"Whoa," Ace said. The geek had paused in whatever he was doing on the tablet, watching the old Viet with intelligent analysis.

"That's rough," Bobby said in a gruff basso. "Phong probably knows a lot that happens around here. Does he know anything about Diep's main operation, though? Anything that's useful?"

"Adequate," *Anh Long* said. "An intelligence network, a good one, is able to piece together information from multiple sources, in order to obtain an objective."

Bobby grabbed the back of one huge arm, massaged it. "Doubt I could stand in the same room with the man that deprived me of a grandkid."

A flash of pain crossed the Elder Dragon's features. He looked at Bobby. "We are playing for futures. It's the war that must be won, not the battles. Sacrifices have to be made. Even of my own." He cleared his throat, suddenly looking older. "Intelligence on the enemy is more valuable than revenge. And whenever you can employ a former enemy they are surprisingly reliable."

So that's why Phong didn't have his crew rush the boutique, I thought. *He was holding back on purpose.*

I chuckled. Everyone looked at me. I remarked sarcastically, "Reliable. Phong reliably shot me in the leg."

Patty thought that was hysterical and brayed a horrible laugh. I turned and watched her, then heard Shocker let loose an amused squeal. I twisted to glare at her, *It wasn't that funny.* She held her face and wheezed. In seconds everyone was laughing. Even the kids. I scowled at the men, at my girl. "Hey! That shit wasn't funny!"

They laughed harder. Shocker pointed at my leg and fell back against the wall.

Patty was seated in the bedside chair with Jasmine in her lap. When the raucous subsided, she twirled a hand above her head and said, "So when's the party starting? Guess I'll fill in for Gisele here." She indicated Blondie, then looked at Shocker. "That's what you really wanted me here for, right?"

The girl-beast nodded, then looked at me. *Patty's competent, and we need her.*

I gestured, *Cool. Good.*

Patty eyed each of us and stated with excited attitude, "'Bout time! I'm sick of babysitting while you have all the fun."

Blondie had turned her head, glowering at Patty, ignoring the pain it caused her. She didn't like being replaced, and liked being compared to Gisele even less. It was a compliment if you asked me – she looked like the athletic sister of the famous supermodel. But she hated it. Her bruised and drugged, but still gorgeous, eyes shot daggers at Patty, *I'm BLONDIE goddamnit!*

Smirking, I told Patty, "Party doesn't start until we have more information."

Usually this would cue my girl, the researcher of our partnership. But since we were a crew now and her talents had been needed in the field, the research gig was all on the geek. I looked at him expectantly.

Ace squinted one eye and glanced around. "You guys may be interested in the local news first."

"About what happened yesterday?" Bobby said.

Ace said, "Uh-huh. SWAT captured everyone that attacked the boutique. Three were shot, one killed. Phong was released a couple hours ago on a million dollar bond."

Surprised murmurs and curses erupted. Despite the revelation about Phong supplying intelligence, no one liked him. I looked at *Anh Long* with a quizzical frown, *You bail him out?*

No, he shook his head, eyes shifting in bafflement.

"Diep must need him for something important," Shocker said in a careful tone, suppressing emotion to avoid upsetting the baby on her hip. She met my eyes. "His position could be useful to us."

"I think so too," I replied, storing that bit of interesting data.

Anh Long was thinking furiously. He became frustrated, mad that his analysis was flawed. "I was under the impression Phong was expendable. Hmm." He pinched his chin. "Perhaps Diep feels Phong's actions yesterday proved a strong loyalty to the Tiger Society, deserving of a promotion."

"Or perhaps he's getting low on men with fully functional arms and legs," I said, thinking about all the guys my crew had beat the crap out of. I smiled to myself, then gestured for Ace to continue.

He said, "I've been trying to track Vietech. I figure wherever he is, Diep must be close by, right? I found some leads." He pressed on the tablet's screen and scrolled through something without looking at it. He said to Blondie, "I took the liberty of tracing anyone that wasn't a regular customer to the boutique and coffee service. In the past few days I found only two new customers. One used an Internet protocol out of New Orleans."

"What?" Blondie croaked, eyes widening. She shifted around like she wanted to sit up. I stepped over and lay a hand on her shoulder. Her big glistening eyes looked up at me helplessly. I said quietly, "I know you want to do your part. Just give it a few days." I stroked her hair over one ear. She closed her eyes, sighing a moan.

Ace continued. "I thought that was something worth investigating so I ran a program that tracked the IP through your website, to see what they had accessed. They had compromised your hard drives, in every store."

Blondie's eyes shot open. "*Shit,*" she breathed vehemently.

Ace nodded at her in sympathy. "Some nasty malware. I can debug it later for you if you want."

"No, I'll do it," she sighed.

I said, "It's public knowledge the Draganflies we used to scald them belong to the coffee service. They would have found the boutique even if Big Guns' boys didn't flip." I felt like stomping my foot and throwing a tantrum.

Blondie knew how much I disliked mixing our legit interests with our criminal ventures. She found my hand and communicated with a squeeze and pout, *We didn't have a choice at the time.*

I know, I squeezed back, then relaxed.

Ace had more good news. He informed us, "The virus Vietech infected her site with gives him full control of everything. He can overwrite any command you give the Draganflies."

I gestured in frustration. "Wonderful. So if we use them anytime soon he can turn them against us. How inconvenient."

You'll have to revise the plan... my subconscious grumbled.

"Damn that guy." I clenched a fist.

"I have something for you," *Anh Long* told Ace. He dug a slip of paper out of his pocket, handed it to the geek. "Cell phone numbers for my men in the Tiger Society. A few will have been in Diep's inner circle at times. They are never told what one another are working on, but tracing their movements as a whole could give us something tangible."

"Right," Ace muttered, studying the numbers, committing them to his extraordinary memory. "I can trace the GPS signals. There will be records of all their movements, dating back to the activation of the phones. We'll know everywhere they went and how long they stayed there. I might be able to extrapolate where Carl and Tho are being held. And any other captives. There are a substantial number of variables. I'll make a chart, and work on equations with –"

"Sweetie," Shocker interrupted. She smiled apologetically to the room, then looked at him with a mild rebuke, *Stay focused.*

"Yes dear," he muttered, then told *Anh Long*, "We can use these." Hues of pink tinged his face as Bobby and Patty snickered. He pocketed the numbers and typed rapidly on his tablet.

"Excellent." I folded my arms. What started as a mission to liberate our Coast from idiotic gang business has turned into something mind-blowing in scope. This was no longer a local or even national problem we faced. If we succeed in shutting down Diep's distasteful operation of profiting from slaves, we'll have done a service for people all over the world.

Who'd a thought a guy like me would become a humanitarian?

A grin slowly stretched my cheeks, and I swear my canines lengthened by an inch. I held a palm up, blew on imaginary dice, and mimed throwing them. *"Challenge,"* I said. A stab of exultant energy raced along my spine.

* * *

The security of our garage in Pass Christian was iffy, and we sure as hell weren't going to the apartment in Gulfport (we just moved there. I wasn't about to chance compromising it already, fuck you very much). So we decided to make our base at Eddy's house. It belonged to Perry now, though I would always think of it as my coach's home.

The beach on our right was devoid of people, sand a dirty white beyond the sea wall, patches of tall grass growing on small dunes. Tiny waves crested and foamed at low tide. Shallow pools and sand bars visible in the sediment-clouded water trapped minnows that were

feasted on by swooping, pooping seagulls. I watched a few of the scav-
engers dive and catch, flying off with tiny fish wriggling death throws
in their sharp, smiling beaks. Then turned my attention from the beach
to Eddy's long steep driveway, Patty next to me in the driver's seat, the
three kids in the back, her Buick SUV humming effortlessly up the hill.

The towering clean white two-story looked just as it did when we
visited a few months ago. Though the landscape of ancient oaks and
rose gardens was far less picturesque than it was in the summer. The
wide circular drive in front of the garage resembled a drag strip pit
area, populated with old and new performance machines that made
my breath catch and goosebumps erupt on my neck.

As the only two-wheeler in the bunch, my Hayabusa really stood
out. I had been worried about the big Suzuki in a way I imagine a
parent frets over a favorite daughter that is late coming home. My
eyes raked its gray and white fairing, polished wheels and suspension, seeking damage. I managed, just barely, to contain myself from
shouting "'Zuki!" and diving out to embrace her. I gave Blondie's truck
a perfunctory inspection. The midnight purple '52 Ford was a show
stopper, with an impressive train of bling lining the pavement on the
other side of it: Perry's bright orange '49 GMC truck; Shocker's hell-
fuck-yeah '59 El Camino, low and mean, red and gray; Big Guns' lime
green otherworldly Honda Prelude; and Ace's Scion FR-S, with a liquid
crystal exterior capable of being the ultimate color scheme – invisible.

Not a pit area, I mused. *It's a special equipment convention.*

"That your bike?" Patty asked as we got out, closed the doors.

"Yep." I started walking over to it.

"Take me for a ride sometime?"

I turned to look at her. She held her hands apart, right fist rolling
an imaginary throttle, left gripping a clutch. She squinched her eyes,
bit her bottom lip, and leaned over as if taking a corner at Gran Prix
speed, making sounds like a motorcycle shifting gears.

Ha! my subconscious chortled. *She would dwarf you on the bike, and
Blondie would tax you for violating the Rule of Bitch Seat: only the blonde
furred crotch of my woman shall warm my passenger seat.*

"I'm not good with passengers," I said. "I have a Blondie-only policy, if you know what I mean. Big Guns has a couple of fast Honda CBRs. If you just want a hundred-ninety miles an hour thrill ride we can arrange that, no problem. Maybe Bobby will take you for a ride."

"A motorcycle ride, or a," she rotated her hips suggestively, "Patty-cycle ride?"

"You'll have fun asking him," I laughed.

"Mommy will you show me how to dance like that?" Jasmine said, trying to watch her mom while supervising Nolan, who got Caroline out of her car seat and shut the door.

Patty's face lost a little color. She was thinking fast. "Jas, you're not, um, old enough to learn that dance yet. One day, yeah, but I, huh. *No...*"

Nolan and I shared a mirthful look. He led the girls inside, leaving me alone with my bike. I ran my hand over the seat, cowhide with the short hair still on it, smooth and feather soft, dyed a dark blonde. My hair stroking turned into a perverted fondling so I quit before anyone caught me. I squatted down and studied the engine, inhaling an intoxicating mix of synthetic oils and high octane fuel, 'Zuki's beastly scent. The Yoshimira exhaust pipes were discolored where they bolted to the cylinder head, hues of blue and gold that would become a glowing orange thousands of degrees hot after the two hundred horses were put through their paces. The fat mufflers themselves, one on each side of the wide rear tire, gleamed like silver, obsessively polished to a mirror finish by my own hands. My reflected image distorted as I inspected their mounting brackets and weld seams. A seesaw, fluffy-numbing euphoria started in my throat and chest, cascading down my torso, lightening my step.

I sighed. "Thought I'd have to break you out of the impound again." One last pinch and twist of the seat, then I turned my full attention to the Ford.

In the shadow of the house the purple paint looked closer to black, shiny glossy surface gray where it reflected the Hayabusa on one side, dull orange where it mirrored Perry's truck on the other. The Ford was wide and low, bed rails below my chest, giving me clear view of my drone in the back.

Demonfly's wings were detached and laying alongside the fuselage, the plane's tail and tips of wings sticking out the open tailgate, far too long for the eight foot bed. She was modeled after the Mitsubishi Zeros the Japanese used in World War II. Unfortunately, I feared my little spy plane would share the same fate as the Kamikaze bombers.

"We didn't get much time to get to know one another," I told the flying demon chick airbrushed on the matte black engine cover. It took me several days of layering and drying to paint her. I was attached to all my art, especially projects as involved as Demonfly. "Our short affair was good for me. How about you?"

"And you called me a thespian *lon*," Big Guns said with his silver smile, walking around the corner of the garage. *"Qui xu,"* psycho. "I knew you'd be out here talking to your machines."

I looked at him. "You get what I need?"

His cheeks widened, teeth gritted. He complained, "Sure. Don't open with 'thanks'. It was no trouble at all to get your bike, truck and plane here. And then," he gestured in outrage, "you had me go shopping! *Du ma,* Razor. Do I look like a Mexican???"

I tagged him in the shoulder with a knuckle. "Well, you *do* eat at Taco Bell a lot…"

He chuffed a reluctant laugh.

"Look. I'm sorry. Thank you for being such a useful burro." I flashed my #1 Mr. Motherfucker smile. "You feel appreciated now?"

He grunted, *Fuck you.*

"Good. Now that you've vented your inner drama queen, let's talk about the job."

He put hands on waist and grunted, *Fine.*

"So did you get what I asked for?"

He showed me a look I could only describe as diabolical. "Oh yeah." He grimaced. "You sure you don't want anything with more kick? Give me a few days and I can score some real fireworks."

Henry Roi

"Nah. We don't have a few days." We turned with silent consent, walked the sidewalk to the front door. Went inside. "Did *Anh Long* get us more men?"

The Viet underboss gave a different kind of grimace, nodding. "They're flying out of San Francisco. California boys." His jaw flexed. He grunted, "*Cac.*"

"I doubt they're thrilled to be coming to Mississippi. We'll need them, in an case." We stopped in the living room. It was empty. My eyes strayed to the huge trophy case, ears becoming aware that everyone seemed to be in the dining room or kitchen.

"Need them as pawns, you mean."

"Pawns, cannon fodder, expendable. That's what *Anh Long* pays them for. They know the score. We need a team of guys we can throw at Diep as a distraction. They'll appear to be our main force, throwing a feint so we can nail their ass in the confusion."

"Too bad we don't have suits and helmets for them." His eyes squinted, one finger tapping on his folded arms, face gold in the lamp light.

"They have vests. We'll make sure the casualties are minimal. It's going to be a siege. Offense chooses the initial level of aggression. We'll have them press just enough to convince Diep it's our primary attack, but not so much they get slaughtered in a counter."

Pursing his lips, his eyes shifted in serious thought. Having nothing to add he said, "I'll leave the war strategy to you." He looked at his watch. "They should land soon. I'll go meet them. We linking up in N.O.?"

"Yeah."

"See you there, bro." We gripped hands, bumped chests, and he left.

I walked through the kitchen, an undefined sense of dread putting me in a state of caution. *Why is everyone suddenly quiet?* I turned into the dining area. Shocker, Bobby and Patty stood over Ace, who sat at the long table with his tablet in front of him, all eight eyes staring at the screen in shocked horror. The kids were clamoring to see, and Perry was moving quickly to corral them, inviting them to watch a

153

movie upstairs. He put on a smile and spoke in a comforting tone, managing to shoo Nolan and Jasmine out of the room, Caroline on his hip with wide eyes and a whiny mouth. They hadn't made it out of earshot before a child's terrified voice screamed from the tablet's speaker. Caroline echoed it, her scream fading as Perry hurried up the stairs. I rushed over to the table.

"Oh my God," Shocker whispered, eyes distraught, welling with tears, as we watched Tho and Carl being struck by a pot-bellied Asian man.

Crack! The man hit the crying boys in turn, open-handed blows that swelled and reddened their dirty, tear-streaked faces, witnessed in gruesome high-definition. Their agonized screams increased in volume, and a dizzying panic blanketed me. Abruptly lightheaded, I leaned over to grip the edge of the table, peering closer at the tablet through a film of scarlet.

The man's head was out of view, his bare, obese torso and stumpy arms all we could see in the light, room dim behind the boys. Carl and Tho were hanging limply, exhausted, their hands bound with archaic manacles above their heads, attached to some kind of apparatus that looked like it could be used for hanging beef. I shut my eyes tightly. The boys were naked, traumatized.

I gripped the table harder, head swimming with vertigo. The scene was macabre, sick and twisted. It showed what kind of person Diep truly was. My eyes shot open and glared at the man that taunted the boys in guttural Vietnamese, talking to them like misbehaving dogs. *This is the kind of people Diep befriends…* We were dealing with a real psychopath.

The urge to snatch the tablet up and break it over my knee was hard to resist. Before I could give voice to my rage the tormentor moved the camera. The adjustment showed only his lower body and the boys' legs. Their ankles were cuffed with manacles so old they were rusted and pitted, iron dating to the days before slavery was outlawed. Streams of blood were dried to their feet, skin cut deeply from struggling, chains anchoring them to the filthy stone floor.

The man reached up and pulled something on the apparatus that brought Tho's and Carl's outstretched arms down, bodies now bent at ninety degrees, bleeding, battered faces suddenly back on the screen. They yelled hoarse, bone-chilling pleas as the man began to take his pants off, cries becoming hysterical when his short erect penis sprang free under his fat stomach.

"NO!" Shocker roared, voice booming with violence. We all flinched. She turned away from the table as a different creature, snarling frighteningly, and punched the nearest wall with a blur of destruction, knocking huge holes in the sheetrock, several framed pictures shattering on the floor. Bobby and Patty lunged and grabbed her, straining to hold her arms, wrestling the berserk woman to the floor with great effort. Ace darted from his seat to help, yelling to get through to his wife.

The commotion behind me felt distant. I stared at the tablet with a stunned detachment, furiously thinking of some way to stop this. Realizing I could do nothing was hard to accept. My throat felt like someone was strangling me. I sat in the vacated chair. Right as the man finished stepping out of his pants the scene changed, obviously to a different room, showing a man and woman of middle age on their knees with their hands tied behind them, battered faces shining sickly with blood and sweat, tears. *Who the hell???* Even clothesless and beaten they looked upper-class, heads held high, regal, the kind of people who could afford procedures to stay youthful in appearance; toned and tanned, no gray or sagging features in evidence. *Their fitness is the only reason they still have composure,* I analyzed coldly.

The camera swiveled to the left, zooming in on a figure I instantly recognized. A growl bubbled deep in my chest at the sight of Diep. When he stuck his face in the camera and spoke I realized this wasn't a recording-

It was live!

"Razor. A pleasure to see you looking so uncomfortable," the Elder Tiger said in a low clear voice. He held up his injured arm. The cast had been replaced with a wrist brace, the hand still healing from the round Loc had put through it months ago. "I'm doing better, thank you for asking."

"Still popping Loratabs, huh? Be careful of addiction," I warned the punk.

His yellow-brown face darkened as he moved closer, the camera shadowing his chin beard and cruel mouth, epicanthic eyes narrowed to evil slits. "Still the crude barbarian, I see," he countered. "Very well. Let us be barbaric." He moved his head slightly toward the captives. "Everything I know about you tells me you don't know these people."

I stared at him, wishing I could tear off his smug jaw from his face and gnaw on it like a chew toy.

He lifted his head a couple feet above the camera and stared down at me, eyes widening with lack of sanity, smile wider. "Ah... You *don't* know them." He danced his head side to side as if to peer around me, humming an upbeat tune. He stopped and suddenly snarled, "Perhaps you're woman knows them."

He moved away from the camera and I could see the couple again. I cringed, heart missing a beat. I could see it now.

I could see Blondie...

That's my girl's freaking parents!

Diep cackled at my stricken expression. He turned toward his captives. He wore a rain suit, bright yellow with tall black rubber boots.

Why a waterproof suit? I pondered. Then, *Damn. It's a blood proof suit...*

Digging in a pocket, he produced a pair of large clear safety glasses, put them on. He studied Blondie's parents dispassionately, like a carpenter studies a wall he must dismantle as part of a larger job. With casual posture he told me, "Once upon a time my tastes were more like my associate's, not quite refined, seeking gratification from choice cuts of young meat. However," he dug in another pocket and pulled out a large knife, unsheathed it, "I've matured."

The woman lost her composure and cried out at the sight of the blade. The man mumbled unintelligible pleas for his wife, his jaw broken severely. Diep dropped the sheath on the floor, stepped forward and contemptuously kicked the man in the stomach, then, in one deft movement, he spun on a toe and swung his arm down gracefully, slicing the knife across the woman's face.

The bound man slumped forward, gasping and coughing with his forehead on the floor. The woman shrieked once, shuddering with silent sobs after that. Her cheek was bathed in scarlet. The deep cut flowed, unceasing, covering her neck, left breast. Her eyes and nose were running. Slowly, she crumpled over and lay on her husband' s back.

Diep smiled down at them. His head rotated to me. He held the knife up, polished steel reflecting the camera and man behind it, wetted with innocent blood. He spoke like we were old friends sharing a beer. "You and I aren't that different, you know."

I wanted to cut this short. I heard myself say, "Well, I still have my Johnson so…"

His eyes locked onto mine, neck rigid, body frozen. Bright insanity radiated from his dark eyes. For a moment I thought I had fucked up, fearing he would turn and start hacking up Blondie's folks. The moment of crazed tension left his face and I remembered to breathe.

He shook his head and knife, *Tisk-tisk,* then told me, "We are both artists. Innovators. We even use similar tools and safety gear," he tapped the tip of the knife on his glasses, leaving spatter on the lenses, "differing only in our methodology: you creatively piece things together. I creatively take things apart."

Heavy breathing suddenly materialized at my side. I glanced at the Shocker, feeling extreme, feverish heat emanating from her body, her sweaty, enraged expression. Her eyes were alight with battle lust, voice husky and threatening. "I'll creatively take *you* apart," she promised Diep.

He lowered the blade and gestured, smiling as if seeing an ex-girlfriend. "Ah! Hello Clarice Ares! Nice to see you haven't been arrested by the FBI and carted back to prison." He cocked his head to one side. "How's Alan Carter? Is your husband still a criminal hacker?"

"I'm here, you fried transistor," Ace spat, appearing over her shoulder. Bobby and Patty crowded behind me, glaring at the tablet with folded arms.

"And your wondrous friends!" The Elder Tiger waved the knife cheerily at Patty and Bobby. "Hello! I've heard so much about you. Will you be joining Razor, Clarice and Alan in the afterlife?"

"There is no afterlife, you worm," Patty said, talking to Diep like he was the biggest moron she'd ever met. Then she growled, "As you'll soon find out."

"That's right, Prickless," Shocker huffed through gritted teeth. She stuck her face up to the tablet and assured our enemy, "*We're coming for you.*"

Dear reader,

We hope you enjoyed reading *A Long Ride*. Please take a moment to leave a review in Amazon, even if it's a short one. Your opinion is important to us.

Discover more books by Henry Roi at

https://www.nextchapter.pub/authors/henry-roi

Want to know when one of our books is free or discounted for Kindle? Join the newsletter at http://eepurl.com/bqqB3H

Best regards,

Henry Roi and the Next Chapter Team

The story continues in :

Criminals by Henry Roi

To read the first chapter for free, head to:
https://www.nextchapter.pub/books/criminals

About the Author

Henry Roi was born and raised on the Mississippi Gulf Coast, and still finds his inspiration in its places and people.

As a GED tutor and fitness instructor, working both face to face and online, he is an advocate of adult education in all its forms. His many campaigning and personal interests include tattoo art, prison reform and automotive mechanics.

He currently works in publishing, as an editor and publicist. He particularly focuses on promoting talented indie writers – arranging reviews, delivering media campaigns, and running blog tours.

If you're not lucky enough to catch him fishing round the Biloxi Lighthouse or teaching martial arts in your local gym, he can usually be found on Twitter or Facebook, under Henry Roi PR.

A Long Ride
ISBN: 978-4-86747-010-7

Published by
Next Chapter
1-60-20 Minami-Otsuka
170-0005 Toshima-Ku, Tokyo
+818035793528
14th May 2021

Lightning Source UK Ltd.
Milton Keynes UK
UKHW012144270521
384511UK00001B/126